WHERE YOUR LOYALTIES LIES 2

A Novel By
KC MILLS

© 2016
Published by Leo Sullivan Presents
www.leolsullivan.com

-1-

"Yo bruh, date's over." Logic pointed to the door making sure to keep eye contact with whoever this Rah dude was. He was pissed with Nova for bringing him to his mother's house, but more than anything, he really wanted to snatch Joy up. It was painfully evident, that she knew Rah, and in an intimate way. That was clear based on the way that Rah was eyeing her body, with a damn smirk plastered all over his face. He was remembering Joy, not just meeting her for the first time. Logic could see it in his eyes, which had every warning sensor in his body going off, and it wasn't in a good way.

"Bruh, no disrespect, but unless she tells me to leave, I'm not going anywhere." Rah looked at Nova. He really didn't care what she thought, but Rah wasn't about to lose the chance to be around Joy again, especially under the current circumstances. He could tell from Logic's reaction that they were together, and it pissed Rah off to see it. He was good with Joy being with Ced's square ass, because Rah knew that Joy would never be serious about a guy like that. But Logic was a different story. Logic appeared to be cut from the same cloth as Rah, and that had him wanting to find a way to put an end to the two of them real quick. Rah knew that Joy could potentially have feelings for Logic, and that wasn't about to happen, not on his watch.

Rah was only really messing with Nova because she was good in bed, and put up with whatever time he offered her. Rah had plenty of women that he rotated, and Nova just happened to be one of them.

"You obviously didn't hear me." In a matter of seconds, Logic's hand was on his gun and he was taking steps towards Rah. Rah in turn followed suit, and had his hand on his gun. Nova saw the situation escalating, so she quickly jumped in between them with her back to Rah, while facing Logic. She had only been kicking it with Rah for a couple weeks, so she wasn't sure how he would react or what he was capable of, but her cousin was a different story. She knew that if Logic actually removed his gun, he would not hesitate to pull the trigger. She had witnessed it for herself several times before, and wasn't about to let that happen tonight. Nova knew that Logic really didn't fear anyone or anything, and he made that very clear more times than she cared to remember. With her hand on Logic's chest to stop him, she spoke over her shoulder to Rah.

"I don't know what's going on, but you need to leave," she spoke firmly, hoping that Rah would get the message.

"Nova, get the fuck out of my way." Logic kept his eyes on Rah while he spoke to Nova, and just before he was about to step around her, he felt hands on his side and heard Joy's voice.

"Logic, please don't. Not in your mother's house."

Joy didn't know what else to do, but she was not about to let either of them allow bullets to fly in Mini's house.

Nova's eyes cut to Joy. Joy saying Rah's name didn't go unnoticed, and she was feeling some type of way about the fact that Joy knew Rah. Just like Logic, Nova could tell from the way Rah was watching Joy, that whatever type of connection they had was far more than just friendship, or the two simply being acquaintances. Logic and Nova had that in common, because he noticed the same thing. Neither of the two were happy about it, but Logic more than Nova was anxious for answers. Right now, however, Rah needed to be dealt with, because he seemed to be feeling himself, which was rubbing Logic the wrong way.

"What the hell is going on?"

Mini's voice made everyone turn towards her. Well, everyone except for Rah and Logic. They were both still staring each other down, Logic's hand under his shirt behind his back and Rah's on his under his shirt but on his waist.

"Nothing Ma, go back in your room," Logic answered, but knew his mother wasn't going for that.

"This is my house, boy, don't tell me where the fuck to go in it." Mini surveyed the situation and instantly picked up on what had her son so heated. She didn't have the details and didn't need them, but the sight of her son standing defensively, with his hand under his shirt on what she knew was a gun, had her heart racing.

"You need to leave," Mini pointed to Rah and then looked at Nova.

"And if you brought him here then you can go too, but either way he's getting out of my house."

Rah finally broke his stare with Logic, when he glanced at Mini and then Nova.

"Yo, hit me up when you get your family bullshit under control." He glanced at Logic and then focused on Joy. "It was good seeing you,

Ma. You look good as always. Don't be a stranger, a nigga's been missing you."

That set Logic off, but this time his gun was in his hand and pointed at Rah's head so quickly, that all he could do was throw his hands up. A smirk spread across Rah's face as he backed up towards the door.

"My bad, bruh. I see she's moved on, I can respect that."

"Auggie, let him go. Don't shoot that man in my house," Mini pleaded with her son. The last thing she wanted was for her son to end up in jail over a female.

Logic could feel his finger trembling from the anticipation of pulling the trigger. Again, Joy placed her hand on him, which caused him to glance at her for a brief moment, but then his eyes were right back on Rah. It was taking every ounce of control he owned not to pull the trigger, but out of respect for his mother, he lowered his gun. Rah winked at Joy, and then walked out the front door. Nova followed behind him and they could all hear her yelling on the porch. This prompted Logic to take a step towards the door, but Mini stepped in front of him.

"Najah, go get her." She pointed towards the door, but kept her eyes on her son, looking at him in away that let him know that he would damn near have to shoot her if he wanted to leave her house.

No one moved except Najah, who obeyed her mother's command and went to go get Nova. A few minutes later, Nova rushed through the door charging right at Joy. "So I guess I was wrong about you, huh? I see you like to play in the streets. I guess my cousin isn't your first time slumming it."

Nova wasn't really mad at Joy; she was just hurt by the way Rah reacted to seeing her. It was clear that there was something there. Even if it was only on his end, there was something there, and that had Nova in her feelings because Rah actually had her thinking that they had something. It had only been a few weeks, but she was feeling him and now all that was over. Logic had beef with Rah, and there was no way he was going to be okay with her dealing with him, and even if he was, she knew enough to know better than to sleep with the enemy.

Before Joy could address Nova's attack, Logic stepped to Nova. "You need to calm all that shit down. Don't come at her 'cause you chose a nigga that's disrespectful." Logic was pissed about the whole situation, but he still wasn't about to let Nova come at Joy because Nova messed around and chose a nigga that wasn't shit.

"Really Logic, you're taking her side?" Nova pointed at Joy while she glared at Logic.

"I'm not taking sides. I don't give a fuck about any of this, but what I am saying is that you need to check that nigga and not Joy."

Joy was annoyed that Logic was trying to handle the situation like she couldn't speak for herself, so she quickly added her two cents to the conversation, since it was about her anyway.

"I dated him, but I didn't know you then and you didn't know me. It's not like I stepped to your man while you were with him. You can't be upset with me about that, the same way I can't be upset with you for being with him now. That's my past and trust me, that's not about to change." Joy didn't need Logic speaking for her, and she wasn't about to hide behind him. Joy didn't care how Nova felt about the fact that she had history with Rah. It wasn't her business, just like it wasn't Joy's that Nova was with him now. Hell, in fact, she hoped that Nova and Rah were happy, at least then she didn't have to worry about him trying to find a way back into her life again.

"You don't have to explain shit to her. Let's go."

"Auggie, you don't need to go anywhere. Not until you calm down. I don't need you doing something dumb over a female." Mini glanced at Joy, but didn't really care how Joy felt about it. Her son was more important than Joy's feelings.

"I love you Ma, but this shit don't have anything to do with you, so mind your business." He stepped around Joy and kissed his mother before he walked towards the door. Nova and Najah both narrowed their eyes at Joy, but she didn't care. They could be mad all they wanted. It wasn't their business either, and she didn't owe them any explanations about her past.

"Let's go!" Logic's voice caught her off guard because of the intensity behind his words. Without saying so much of a goodbye to either of the women whose eyes were burning a hole through her, she followed Logic out the door, dreading what was coming next.

For about the first ten minutes of the drive, neither of them said a word. Logic was still pissed about the fact that Rah tried him, and although he had feelings about the connection Rah had with Joy, he was also processing the fact that Donte's situation with Rah, had become his situation with Rah. Add Joy to the equation, and the situation had just gotten about ten times worse.

"You don't want to talk about it?"

The sound of Joy's voice caused Logic to turn towards her, but he didn't speak. He felt his jaw tighten, while he gripped the steering wheel. He didn't say a word, he just laughed sarcastically under his breath and then focused on the road again. Once they made it to Joy's apartment complex, he parked along the curb instead of in a parking place, so Joy knew he wasn't staying. She opened the door to get out and started towards the door, moving quickly because she was pissed off. She respected the fact that Logic was upset about how things went down, but she also needed him to respect the fact that she had no control over Rah showing his ass.

"Joy!" Logic's voice behind her caused her to stop and turn to face him. When he caught up with her, he looked her right in the eyes.

"The fuck you stomping around for, like I did some shit to you? If anybody deserves to be upset right now, it's me."

Joy laughed. "You sound crazy. You deserve the right to be mad that my ex is dating your cousin, and was disrespectful to her and me?"

Now it was Logic's turn to laugh. "You're so fucking childish. I need you to see past your own bullshit. I don't give a fuck about him being with Nova, but what I do care about is the fact that, that nigga clearly felt the right to address your ass the way he did. I can't say shit about your past, just like you can't say shit about mine, but what went down tonight don't have shit to do with your past. That nigga's feelings were current as a motherfucker, so tell me why I get the feeling that he has a reason to think that way?"

"If you're insinuating that I'm still messing with him, then you're wrong."

"I ain't insinuating shit Joy. I'm straight up asking you. Are you still fucking with that nigga?"

Joy just laughed. She stared at Logic, not believing that they were even having this conversation. In fact, she wasn't going to have this conversation, so she just turned to walk away. She stopped briefly when she heard his voice behind her. "You walking away is your answer, but trust me, if you walk away it's not just for tonight, so think about that before you keep moving."

"Yeah, well it doesn't really matter anyway does it, because you have apparently already made up your mind. Good night Logic."

Just like that, Logic stood on the sidewalk watching as Joy's door shut, separating the two of them. As much as he wanted to go after her, he just couldn't, not right now anyway. He didn't know if he would at all, but for now, he needed to go see Gotti. Logic had a feeling that tonight wasn't going to be the last he heard of Rah, because the second Rah realized that Logic had taken Donte's place, they were going to have a war on their hands.

When Logic pulled up on his block, he surveyed his surroundings. He could see things that most people would miss because they didn't know their system. A few of his guys were sitting on the stairs talking, while others were moving in the shadows, serving customers. It looked like things were under control, but Logic still needed to have a conversation with Gotti. Before he could get out of his car, his phone was going off, so he pulled it out of his pocket. It was his sister, and his first reaction was to ignore the call, but he knew she would keep calling if he did, so he decided to get it out the way.

"What Najah?"

"Don't come at me like that, I'm not the one. And your little bullshit attitude needs to be directed at Joy and not me. I didn't do shit to you, Auggie."

"Najah, I don't have time for this shit right now. I'm busy."

"Busy doing what Auggie? Mommy might not know, but I do. I know you're back in the streets."

"You don't know shit, so mind your business and keep your damn mouth shut." Logic knew that it was just a matter of time before his mother realized what he was doing, but he wasn't ready for that conversation just yet. It wasn't going to change anything, but he still didn't want her to worry about him.

"She's going to find out Auggie, hell, she might already know, but if not, it's only a matter of time. I saw it coming, so I know she did too."

Logic was quiet for a minute, processing what his sister was telling him, when he noticed Gotti walking to his car, and knew that he had to cut his conversation short.

"It's who I am Nah Nah. I know it's not the best choice, but it's the one for me. I know Ma is not going to like it, but I gotta do what works for me."

"I know that, and she's never going to be okay with it, but she'll figure out a way to live with it. Just be safe Auggie. I can't lose you too, I just can't."

"I'm good Najah, I promise you that, but I have to go. I'll come check you out in a few days."

"I love you Auggie."

"I love you too."

Logic ended the call with his sister and tried to let the conversation go. He couldn't function if he let his emotions get the best of him, so he shut that part of his mind off for now, the same way he left his thoughts about Joy behind when he left her at her apartment. It wasn't like he wasn't going to deal with her, but for now his focus was business. He had to get used to separating the two, so that he didn't get caught slipping. Emotions made you vulnerable, and that was a sure fire way to end up on the wrong end of a bad situation.

"What's up Logic?"

Gotti waited patiently for him to get out of his car. The two men walked up the steps of their stash house, being careful to survey their surroundings. It was necessary to always make sure that they were aware of everything going on around them.

"Rah is going to be a problem for us." Logic wasted no time getting right to the point.

Gotti read Logic's expression noticing the seriousness behind it, and assumed that the two must have had a run in.

"Did he come at you?" Gotti asked.

"Not yet, but he will. He doesn't know who I am yet, but we share a common interest, and I have a feeling that's going to make him come for me, which means that he will be coming for us."

"Is there anything I need to know?" Logic was being vague, but Gotti trusted him enough to be okay with that.

"He has history with my girl, and I just found out tonight. Let's just say that shit didn't go well, and the second he connects the dots, that this is me..." Logic nodded towards the house they were in. "Then he's coming for anything I have which means this."

"It's whatever," was all that Gotti said. That was enough explanation for him. He was ready to defend their territory at all costs, and he would stand beside Logic with whatever decisions he made. He trusted Logic and knew that he would do whatever was necessary. Logic had always been fair, and he treated his team like family, so Gotti saw no reason not to return the favor. Logic was family, which meant that Gotti would take on his situations as if they were his own.

"We need to make sure everyone is on the same page. Let's meet tomorrow. I want everyone on point. If Rah's people are coming for us, we need to be prepared."

"Aight, I'm good with that. You heading out?"

"Nah, I'm going to hang around here for a minute and check things out. You got the deposits ready?"

"Yeah, money's looking good. I'm telling you Logic, just your name alone is bringing business. Shit picked up immediately."

Logic followed behind Gotti to the back of the house, through the kitchen and into the basement. He moved a shelf away from the wall, opened the safe that was in it, and pulled out a book bag that he handed over to Logic. Logic surveyed the stacks of money, and did a mental count. He was so used to counting money that he could usually get an accurate count without even putting his hands on it.

"This for the week?" Logic asked.

"Hell no, for the last two days. I told you shit is moving," Gotti said with a grin.

Logic felt that rush again, from being in a position of power. He missed it. No matter how much he tried to deny it, the streets held his heart.

He kicked it with Gotti and Lil Chris for a a few more hours, before he eventually decided to head home. It was late and he was tired. The downside to that was that heading home meant the return of thoughts about Joy, and they were heavy on his mind again. He missed her no matter how much he tried not to, and that was fucking with him because he needed her. After such a short time, he needed her, and in a way that he knew wasn't going to be easy to erase from his life.

Logic dragged himself from his car and to his door. Key in hand, he let himself in and didn't bother turning on any lights. Every inch of his apartment was embedded in his memory, so he didn't need lights to find his way.

Once he was in his room, he turned on the lamp that sat in the corner and smiled when he noticed Joy asleep in his bed. As much as he wanted to be mad at her, just seeing her in his bed gave him as sense of peace that he hadn't realized he was missing.

Unfortunately, that was clouded by the events of the evening, so he couldn't even enjoy it. Instead of dealing with her, he removed his clothes and made his way to the closet to put the money he collected from Gotti in his safe. After he had it secure, he collected his things to shower so that he could go to bed. He planned on sleeping on the sofa, because as much as he wanted to feel Joy's body next to him, that wasn't enough. He needed to be sure that what they had wasn't temporary, and Rah had him questioning that. Before leaving his room to shower, Logic stood in his doorway, watching Joy sleep. Her hair was lying across her face, which was contorted into a frown. His body was craving her, but he had to fight against it, at least for now. So after releasing a frustrated breath, he left his room.

-2-

Joy woke up and looked around Logic's room, almost in a daze, until she focused on the fact that he wasn't in his bed. Her heart sank just a little, when the first thought was that he didn't come home. That could have meant a lot of things, but the first thought that invaded Joy's mind, was that he had possibly stayed with another woman.

She and Logic were still new, so she understood that he could have easily found a willing participant to allow him a place to lay his head for the night. Amongst other things, after pulling herself from his bed, she tried to wrap her mind around the fact that she had to somehow survive her day, knowing that things weren't good between the two of them.

After walking away from him, she realized that she hadn't really meant to make such a bold statement, and she was praying that they could have a conversation to fix whatever Rah had broken between them.

Rah. Just thinking about him sent a wave of fire through her body. She couldn't believe how he behaved; well honestly, she could. But for him to act as if they were anything more than a bad decision and a past she didn't want to revisit, had her furious. To add insult to injury, Logic didn't even bother hearing her side. She knew that Logic had trust issues, but for him to just assume that Rah meant something to her, or that she was actually still connected to him, hurt.

After Joy gathered her things and took them to the bathroom, so that she could shower and change, she noticed Logic's keys on his dresser. She was a little confused, because he wasn't in bed with her and she hadn't heard him come in.

Joy did a quick survey of his room, and didn't notice anything out of place, but she wouldn't have realized it anyway, because the only thing she had done when she got there was to get undressed and go to sleep.

The second she reached his living room and found Logic stretched out on his sofa, arms folded covering his face, chest exposed, her heart hurt a little more. He did come home, but didn't care enough to wake her, or even sleep in the same bed.

She stood there watching him sleep for a minute, before she decided go ahead and wake him.

"Why didn't you wake me when you got home?"

Logic opened his eyes and stretched. The displeased look on his face told Joy exactly how he felt about her being there.

"Why are you here?"

Logic stood and stepped around Joy. It took everything he had to do it, because he really wanted to kiss her. Her sad eyes were breaking him, but he wasn't about to put himself out there like that.

"Because I feel like we need to talk," Joy said following behind him.

He laughed sarcastically as he opened his drawer, took out a shirt and then pulled it over his head. He still hadn't made eye contact with Joy.

"Your ass should have wanted to talk last night. I told you that if you walked away then it wasn't just temporary. I have too much shit on my mind to be worried about you playing me for some nigga that you're sharing with my cousin Joy."

His eyes finally made contact with hers, and he could see the reality of the words that just left his mouth, written all over her face. He regretted being so harsh, but the idea of Joy dealing with someone else had him in a place he had never been before. Never once had Logic cared enough that the idea of another man having a connection with someone that he was dealing with mattered, but with Joy, just the thought of her being with Rah had him wanting to put a bullet in him. He didn't understand how she had done that to him so quickly, but it was a luxury that he couldn't afford. He couldn't allow someone to have that much power over him, and not feel as if he could trust them. That was a hazard.

"You didn't really give me a choice. You basically accused me of cheating on you without even really knowing the facts."

"If I recall correctly, I didn't accuse you of shit. I asked you if you were still fucking with that nigga, and you walked off. What the fuck was I supposed to think Joy? I'm not a damn mind reader."

"You shouldn't have had to ask me that. You should have known."

Again, Logic laughed. "What I know is if I didn't have a gun pointed at that nigga, he would have probably been all over your ass, so how do you expect me to look past that?"

"I expect you to know me."

"All due respect Joy, that's not good enough. I gave you a chance to explain, and you wanted to be on some kindergarten shit, stomping around like I didn't have the right to ask you that shit in the first place."

Joy just looked at him not knowing what to say next. They were both quiet. Logic waited for Joy to give him a reason to let her stay, and Joy was trying to figure out how they had even gotten to this point.

"Once again, I guess I'll take that to be your answer. Lock the door when you leave."

He walked out of his bedroom into his bathroom, and slammed the door. He stood here for a minute because he needed to get his mind right, but Joy kept invading his thoughts. He proceeded to wash his face and brush his teeth, and when he was done, he placed both hands on the sink while staring at his reflection. Logic wasn't really sure what he was looking for; in fact, he knew that he was just giving himself a minute, just in case Joy hadn't left yet. Seeing her face made him weak, and he wanted to break down, but then his mind would move to thoughts of Rah.

After getting himself together enough to face her again, he left the bathroom and sure enough, she was sitting on the edge of his bed waiting.

"None of this is helpful. Maybe we made a mistake, but either way I can't really focus on this right now." He decided to speak first.

"Really Logic, is it that easy for you?"

"Why wouldn't it be?" He didn't mean that, and he didn't know why he was acting like it was that simple, because he knew that it would hurt her and that wasn't his intention.

"Fine, I guess it is. For the record, I'm not still dealing with him. I haven't in over a year, but I guess you don't really care about that, so do with it what you want." She walked over to the dresser and lifted her keys. She began removing the key that Logic had given her, but he grabbed her hand and took the keys from her.

"What?" she asked.

Logic smiled even though he hadn't really meant to, but hearing Joy confirm what he was praying to be true, made his heart smile, and it filtered over into his expression. He had what he needed from her. All he ever really wanted was for Joy to tell him that it was just the two of them. It was insane how he needed that confirmation from her, but he did, and he believed her the second the words left her lips.

"Come here." Logic's voice was calm and low but Joy didn't move. She just studied his face, still caught up in his initial reaction.

"I have to get ready for work." Joy stayed put, knowing good and damn well she was aching to be close to him.

"Joy, come here." There was only about a foot's distance between them. Logic could have easily reached for Joy, but he wanted the movement to be her choice, initiated by her. He stood his ground, just like she did, but he could see her breaking with every second that her stubbornness held her in place.

Their standoff eventually ended when Joy could no longer stand the distance between them. How could this man have her so wrapped up? She broke down and took a step towards him, and that was all he needed. With one fluent motion, his hands were on Joy, gently but with force, and she was locked in his embrace while his lips grazed her cheek. The pounding coming from her chest forced her breathing to become labored, even though she tried her best to control it.

"I can't be with someone that I don't trust. Especially not now... everything's different now. I need you to understand that." His breath tickled her senses, as he whispered against her ear.

"You can trust me," Joy said meaning every word. She wasn't going to be disloyal to Logic in any type of way. His presence intimidated her, but not in a way that made her fear him. It simply made her crave him in a way that would make her do anything for him.

"Can I?" Logic's hand cupped the back of Joy's head and she tilted it back just a little, anticipating what was next. Logic couldn't control the smile he felt surfacing at her instincts.

"With your life and every secret you've ever kept." Joy spoke with so much conviction that Logic could no longer control the urge to taste her lips. So he kissed her in a way that let her know that he was accepting her offer of loyalty.

"You need to get dressed. You're about to be late." Logic kissed Joy on the forehead and let her go. Just that quickly, he was back in business mode. She had to be at work and so did he. His first stop was going to be Intrigued. He needed to have a conversation with Luther and after that, he needed to prepare his team for what he felt like was about to happen.

Joy began to sulk. Work was the last thing on her mind, but she prided herself in being responsible, so regardless, she was going. "So, can I see you later?"

"You will see me later," Logic said as he went to get his phone from the living room.

That had Joy beaming just a little, but she still didn't want to go.

"We need to talk. Just call me when you get off." Joy took in Logic's demeanor, noticing the change in him. From the day she first laid eyes on him, she knew that he was a man of action, but right now there was a confidence in him that he owned intimately. It made him even sexier, as if that were possible. She didn't understand how that transformation happened so quickly, but she was sure it had something to do with his recent decision about hitting the streets again. What she was seeing in Logic was one of the qualities that she used to see in Rah years ago, but Logic wore it differently. He had a way about him that had Joy obsessing over him.

Logic's phone went off, bringing Joy out of her thoughts about him. She watched as he held it to the side of his face. Every move he made was sexy to her, without any effort on his part.

"What's good Gotti, we all set?"

Logic left his bedroom to speak privately, but not before blessing Joy with a kiss on the lips that had her heart fluttering. She was in love, no doubt about it.

*****

"Logic, I really need you to think about what you're doing. Think about what it's going to do to your mother."

Logic was half listening to Luther and in fact, the only reason why he was even there was because he had respect for Luther. His mind was made up and the decision had been made, but he felt like he owed Luther, at the very least a face to face, to let him know that his priorities had changed.

"Luther, you know you're my peoples. Shit, you're damn near my father, and I don't ever want you to feel like I don't appreciate that, but this is me. I tried shit your way and it's not working. I'm at home in the streets. It's in my DNA, and I just need you to respect that. But check it, I need a favor."

Luther's hand went across his hair and he studied Logic's face. True indeed this was not his son by blood, but in every other way that mattered. Luther didn't have to like Logic's decision to respect it. Every man had to choose his own path and accept the consequences that were born from it. Logic was not exempt from that, and Luther also knew that Logic understood that.

"What's that son?"

"She needs you. Take care of my mother."

Luther nodded. There were so many different meanings to that statement, but the most important one was that Logic was passing down his duties as the man in his mother's life, to Luther.

"It's already done."

The men shared a quick hug and Luther watched as Logic left Intrigued. His heart was heavy, but he had no choice but to let him go.

When Logic walked into their stash house, he eyed all of his people. They watched him intently, waiting for his guidance. In just days, they had become dependent on his leadership. Logic just had that effect on everyone he came across, but the beauty in it was that he didn't abuse that power. He was honest and fair. If you were loyal to him, then he gave that right back without question, but you would only cross him once. Being honest and fair damn sure didn't make him a fool.

"We're making money. That shit is gonna come regardless, but more important than that, we're regaining the respect we lost because of Donte. If niggas respect you, then they will be less likely to fuck with you. Don't take that to mean that they won't, but respect goes a long way. Rah and his people need to understand that we are together in this. This is our shit and it's gonna stay our shit. You see them coming for you, take a life because they won't hesitate to take yours. Anybody got a problem with that?"

The room was silent, but the flow of eye contact and head nods gave Logic the confirmation that he was looking for.

"Good. Go make some money."

After a few brief words and affirmations, the room was empty again. Lil Chris and Gotti sat across from one another, while Logic stared out the window watching his people work. He was lost in this thoughts. For some reason, he kept thinking about his brother. Maybe it was the fact that he was in the streets again, but either way, Bernard was heavy on his mind. It made his heart hurt a little.

"You good Logic?" Lil Chris offered him the blunt that he was working on, and Logic shook his head turning it down. He needed his mind clear.

"Yeah, what's our inventory looking like?"

"It's time to re-up. I told you that shit is selling."

Logic smiled at the thought of making money, but he was more drawn by the process of it all. It had never been just about material things. He liked nice shit, but it's not what made him tick. The power was what pushed him. There was something about the way people fell in line under his control, or reacted when his name was spoken. That was what he missed the most. The money was just an added bonus.

"Okay, I'll make some calls. I want you there." Logic knew enough to keep his hands clean. He was meticulous about that. Especially now, there was no way he was about to end up in jail, opening the door for another motherfucker to step in and take Joy. He had her and he was keeping her.

"Just let me know, but we got shit to take care of, so if you don't need us—"

"Handle your business," Logic said nodding at Gotti and then Lil Chris. The three men dapped each other before Gotti and Lil Chris hit the front door.

Logic pulled out his phone and shot Joy a quick text.

I miss your lips.

He knew that she was working, so instead of waiting for a reply, he locked his phone and slid it into his pocket. For now, he had work to do.

-4-

Rah watched Nova as she walked towards him. The scowl on her face made him regret the fact that he showed up at her place, but he wanted to fuck, and he also wanted to try and find out what was up with Joy and her cousin.

He knew that once he fed Nova his dick, that she would feed him information.

"What do you want Rahjee? Your ass clearly don't give a fuck about me based on the way you were eye fucking my cousin's girl," Nova snapped, hoping that he would show some signs that he felt something for her.

"Look ma, I don't know what you're thinking, but ain't shit there anymore. Yeah, I admit I was wrong as fuck, but I'm man enough to admit that. You gotta give me a break." Rah removed his body from against his car, where he had been waiting in Nova's driveway. He gripped her waist, and once her body made contact with his, he kissed her lips and then her neck. The connection made his dick hard which she had to notice.

"Yeah, I bet. You just want some pussy," Nova said and then pecked him on the lips.

"I don't have to beg for pussy, ma. You know that. I'm being real with you. Past is the past." Rah pulled Nova further into his body.

"I hope you mean that because Logic don't play about his women," Nova released casually, not really understanding the power of what she was doing. She was feeding right into Rah's plans.

The name Logic struck a nerve with Rah. The streets had been talking, and Logic was the person responsible for Donte and Fez disappearing. Logic was also the name given in connection to who was now running the area of College Park that Rah wanted for himself. *Fuck, this shit is getting better and better.*

"You gonna keep talking, or we gonna take this shit inside so that I can show you where my priorities are?" Rah asked, feeling pleased about his newfound inside track.

"I shouldn't be fucking with you at all, but you know I can't resist." Nova had no intentions of sticking it out with Rah after everything that happened, but what would it hurt to have one more round before she walked away. Rah knew how to work her body and she wanted one last taste.

"I'm a call you later, and don't have your ass in the streets," Rah said as he adjusted his clothes. He had just put a hurting on Nova's body, but now it was time to handle business. He needed to get some information about Logic. Nova was being tight lipped about him, and he couldn't press her without being obvious. But, he did find out that he had just recently started dealing with Joy.

"Boy please, you about to leave me and be up in some other bitch's face, so don't worry about me being in the streets. And besides, I'm about to pick Kenyan and Kenya up for school, and then head to work."

Rah chuckled. If he hadn't seen Joy with Logic, he might have actually considered letting Nova fall into a main spot. Not on some faithful type shit, because that wasn't his thing, but in a way that gave her a regular role in his life. All that was dead though, the moment he laid eyes on Joy again. He wanted her back. Joy was wife material, and he wasn't about to let another nigga have that with her. He'd kill every single one who tried, starting with Logic.

"Play your cards right and I might have something for you," Rah said and winked at Nova, before pulling out his ringing phone.

"Yeah."

"Why aren't you here?" Marilyn's voice annoyed the shit out of him. He was pissed that her dumb ass broke their agreement and told Joy that they were fucking.

"Because I'm where the fuck I am," Rah yelled and then eyed Nova, before he walked out the room and of course, he could hear Nova yelling behind him.

"See, that right there is why you don't need to be worried about me being in the streets. Trifling ass, up in my shit and entertaining another bitch."

"Chill Nova, this ain't another bitch, this is business."

"Mm hmm, and I'm stupid as fuck."

Rah shook his head and focused on Marilyn.

"If you would stop fucking with those young girls that don't know how to appreciate a man like you, you wouldn't have to deal with that type of stress."

"I ain't stressed, and your ass needs to stop acting like you mean something to me, or that you have something that I can't get somewhere else."

"Lie to yourself if you want to, but we both know I do things to you that those young girls can't even dream of."

Rah inhaled and let it out slow. She was right. Marilyn had a way with him, but not so much that he couldn't live without it. In fact, he planned on fucking her a few more times, but once he had Joy in his life again, he was putting an end to that. He refused to let Marilyn ruin things for him.

"Yo, is there a point to this call because I have business to handle?"

"I want to see you tonight. Lionel is out of town for two days so I want you here tonight."

"I'll think about it," Rah said.

Marilyn laughed. "Yeah, okay." She hung up.

Rah couldn't worry about Marilyn right now; he had more important things to do, like hitting the block to get information on Logic and paying Joy a visit. He needed to get her alone. If he could do that, then he knew that he would be able to get under her skin in a way that would show her what she was missing. He needed to prove that he learned from his past mistakes, and was ready to be the man she begged him to be a year ago, even if it was a lie. But Rah knew one thing for sure, and that was that Logic's family would be planning a funeral before he stepped back and let him take what was rightfully his. Joy belonged to him.

*****

"You know you wrong, right?" Nova didn't want to hear anything that Najah was saying, but she knew that Najah was right. She had no reason to be mad at Joy, because Rah's ass was being disrespectful. Hell, she needed to check him, but his dick game was too strong and she wanted it in her life. She hated herself for being so pathetic over a man, but sometimes things just were what they were.

"I don't need you telling me that shit. I'll make it right." Nova rolled her eyes. She was sitting outside her job and had fifteen minutes before her shift was to start.

"Well you better. Auggie likes that girl Nova, and like it or not, she's gonna be around."

"Ain't nobody worried about Auggie. He can kiss my ass," Nova said, knowing that she was just talking. One thing she knew for sure, was not to play around with her cousin. Logic meant business, and she wasn't about to get caught up on his bad side.

"Yeah aight, let him hear you say that," Najah laughed. "But real talk boo, Joy's alright. Hell, she jumped at your ass, so she got a backbone. She didn't seem fazed by that nigga you were with, so don't put that on her. Just a casualty of war, but you better stop messing with him or Auggie is gonna be in your shit."

"Girl bye, I know better." Nova squeezed her thighs still feeling the hurting that Rah had just put on her. She planned on walking away, but only after she had a few more rounds. What would that hurt?

"I'm serious, Nova. Don't get stuck in a situation that will have you fucked up in the game. You know how Auggie is. He's got it out for that nigga and I think it's deeper than Joy."

"I said I know better Najah, damn. Let me have this, but I have to go. My shift is about to start. I'll call you later."

"Aight cuz."

Nova ended the call feeling some type of way. She was torn. The one time she found a decent guy, he had to be off limits because of some shit that didn't even involve her. She let out a frustrated sigh and then got out of her car. For now, she couldn't worry about that. She had a building full of annoying ass customers that she knew were about to piss her off. That, unfortunately, was her current state of mind, meaning everything else would have to be dealt with later.

Rah made it back to his block with Joy on his mind. She was literally all he could think about, and it was really fucking with his head. It had been a year and he managed to stay focused and not really worry about her, as long as he was making money and had plenty of women in rotation. But seeing her changed all that.

"Yo nigga, where the fuck you been?" Moses made his way over to his brother, looking like he was mad at the world. He hated when Rah just disappeared like he had recently just done. Rah was forever letting some female cause him to lose focus. Unlike Rah, Moses was all about making money.

"Why the fuck you charging at me, like I'm one of these little niggas that work for us Moses? I had some shit to do, but it's none of your damn business."

Rah shut his truck door and walked past his brother, making sure he made contact with him. Moses needed to calm the fuck down.

"You always on some shit Rah. Is pussy that important? We're supposed to be handling our shit right now, but you wanna be laid up."

"Didn't I tell you we would get this shit done?" Rah turned and pointed at his little brother, staring him down so intensely that Moses hesitated a little. There wasn't much Moses feared in his life, but he knew better than to challenge his brother. He knew that Rah wasn't playing with a full deck on most days.

"Chill Rah, I'm just saying. If we don't act now, someone else is going to claim Donte's territory and we need that shit. It's supposed to be ours anyway." Moses backed down just a little, not wanting to set his brother off.

"Somebody already beat us to it, but we're gonna take that shit from him so it's all good. Just calm your ass down and tell me what the numbers look like."

Rah entered his four-bedroom house with Moses right behind him. It wasn't the biggest house, but it was nice and he had his shit laid, just the way he liked it. Problem was, Rah wanted more and he needed the territory that Logic was running to make that happen.

"What do you mean somebody already claimed it?" Moses asked, pulling out a blunt that he was mindlessly about to light up, until he heard his brother's voice.

"Don't light that shit in my house. You know my fucking rules, take that outside Moses."

Rah treated his home like a sanctuary. If he didn't smoke in it, no one else was going to. The crazy thing was that all that started because of Joy. She hated when he would have the house filled with smoke, chilling with his boys. She complained so much that he shut all that down. He didn't bring his boys around his home, and even Rah would go outside on the porch to light up. He did it to make Joy happy, but even after she was gone, it had become a habit that he maintained even after they broke up.

"Exactly what I said, nigga. Somebody already claimed it."

"You talking about that Logic motherfucker?"

"If you already knew, then why the fuck you asking me that shit?" Rah asked irritated. He opened the cabinet to get a bottle of Ace out.

Moses laughed. "Fuck him, Rah. He ain't no problem. That nigga writes poems and shit while serving coffee. He can't fuck with us. We'll just take that shit."

"Don't get it confused. He ran that shit with Donte before his brother was killed. He knows his shit from what I hear, and now that he's back, he's got the streets buzzing."

Moses looked at his brother strangely. "You worried about him?"

"Hell no, the fuck I look like. I'm just saying it's not going to be as easy as you think. Donte was a bitch. He couldn't fuck with us, and that's probably why that nigga's not breathing now. Logic knows his shit, but trust me, I got something for his ass. We're gonna start fucking with his people first to get under his skin, and then we're going hard as hell to take that shit."

Rah smiled to himself at the thought of firing on Logic. It was coming, and soon.

"That's what I'm talking about," Moses said.

"But check it. I have a few things to handle and then I'll be back. After that, we can make some moves."

Moses got irritated all over again. He knew his brother was about to go lay up in some female, but he couldn't really say shit about it. Rah did what he wanted to do, and not even Moses could change that. For now, Moses was about to hit the block to check on their people, light up his blunt and hope that his brother would be ready for business later.

"Yeah aight, don't be all night nigga."

"Fuck you Moses, I'll be around when I'm ready to be around. Now get the fuck out of my house so that I can shower and change."

Rah was on his way upstairs to his bedroom, so he didn't bother looking back at his brother. Not long after, Moses was out the door and Rah was in the shower.

When Rah made it to Marilyn's house, he keyed in the security code to let himself in. He chuckled to himself. Her husband was clueless. Rah moved around the house Lionel paid for like he owned it. The same way he fucked his wife like he owned her. Too bad this was going to be the last time. He was going to miss Marilyn a little, but Joy was more important than the occasional nut he got from Marilyn.

"I see you got your shit together and realized where you needed to be," Marilyn said as soon as Rah entered her bedroom. Rah laughed at her horny ass because she had no idea if he was going to show, but she was naked other than the short silk robe that was wide open, exposing her body.

Rah could feel the swell in his jeans as he admired her body. Marilyn was fit as hell for her age and undeniably sexy. He loved that about her. Add in the fact that she had some bomb ass pussy and she was a certified freak, Rah was winning.

Marilyn made her way over to Rah and began unbuckling his jeans. She kept her eyes on him the entire time while Rah admired her beauty. Marilyn was truly easy on the eyes but she wasn't Joy, so when Marilyn had him free and tried to drop to her knees to please him, he stopped her.

"Nah, I don't need that." He lifted her to her feet, pulled her back to his chest as he moved towards the wall. He used his hand to open her legs before sliding in her nice and slow, but that only lasted for a minute. He was there to fuck just one last time before he ended things.

Rah began to punish Marilyn's body, moving in and out of her so roughly that she tried to stop him and gain control of the situation. He laughed and focused on Joy's face in his head, because he was physically with Marilyn but mentally with Joy. It didn't take long for him to nut, and Marilyn was right there with him. She liked it rough, which actually turned her on. She continuously complained about how boring her husband was, if and when they did have sex, so she used Rah as a way to release her pent up frustrations.

"That one was yours but now it's time for me to get mine," Marilyn said when Rah stepped away from her so she could remove her body from the wall he had her pressed against.

He laughed, "Nah, I'm good. I just needed to feel that shit one last time."

Marilyn looked at him like she wanted to slap him. There was no way that she was about to let him walk away. "We're not done, not tonight and not ever."

Rah pointed at her. "You don't have a say in that."

He looked down and began adjusting his clothes.

"Yes I do, and you know it. You don't want to leave me."

"And you don't want me to tell your husband that you're fucking your daughter's ex. This cushy little lifestyle of yours means something to you, and I know it. I guarantee he'll divorce your ass in the blink of an eye if he knew about us."

Marilyn opened her mouth to speak but nothing came out.

"I thought so. I'm getting Joy back, trust me, and if you try to fuck that up again, I will be having a conversation with Lionel. So don't call me, don't text me and we're good. I am gonna miss that shit though."

Rah had a smirk on his face as he winked at Marilyn and turned towards the door. He heard Marilyn behind him but didn't stop.

"I hate you, Rah! Fuck you! Just like I found you, I can find someone else."

He just shook his head and laughed at her old pathetic ass, because he had more important things to do like killing Logic and then getting Joy back.

-5-

"So Rah is fucking with Nova... wow. That's some shit Joy," Karma said through the phone trying to process what her best friend was telling her.

"Girl, you have no idea. I thought Logic was going to shoot him right there in his mother's house, and Nova looked like she wanted to shoot me."

"Oh hell no, cousin or not, she can get it if she's trying to step to you." Karma got heated just thinking about anybody trying to step to Joy. That wasn't happening. Joy wasn't a pushover but Karma was the rowdier one of the two friends.

"Calm down K, I'm not worried about Nova. She'll either get over it or she won't, but I don't care either way." Joy had to laugh at Karma; she was always ready to go in on somebody.

"I'm just saying Joy, we can handle that if we need to," Karma said in all seriousness.

"Nah, we're good."

"So what about Logic? Y'all good or what?"

Joy smiled. "I think so. We kinda had a moment, but I told him there was nothing there and he acted like he believed me. I'm actually getting dressed now to go meet him."

"Shit, he needs to believe you. Fuck Rah and Marilyn's nasty ass. You should have let Logic handle his trifling ass."

"Yeah well, I didn't think it was a good idea for him to be collecting bodies in his mother's living room."

"Collecting bodies. Damn boo, you street already. You sound like you back with Rah again," Karma laughed.

"Kiss my ass. I'm just me, K."

"With a side order of trap queen. You fall into that role too easily boo."

"Whatever, I'm not messing you, it's not like that, but I have to go. I need to hop in the shower real quick."

"Aye, do you boo. Go see your man and get that cat kissed."

"You so damn extra," Joy said and laughed.

"Girl, don't front. I know you 'bout to go get your back blown out," Karma said and then laughed at herself.

"Bye fool. I'll call you tomorrow."

Joy ended the call and collected her things to go shower. She was ready to see Logic. She missed him every second that she was away from him and couldn't wait to feel his body against hers.

When she made it to his place she didn't see his car, so she used her key to let herself in. Joy had stopped to get dinner for the two of them, so her first stop was the kitchen. After setting the Chinese food on the counter, she made her way to his bedroom to unload her overnight bag. Logic hadn't mentioned her staying with him, but he didn't have to. She made the decision for him, assuming that he wouldn't object.

Joy dropped her purse and bag on the dresser before she kicked off her Nikes leaving them in the center of the floor, but only for a minute. Everything in his room was in its place, so seeing her shoes in the center of the floor just felt wrong. After setting them next to his dresser, Joy surveyed his room like it was her first time being in there. She was drawn to the bookshelf that lined the wall overflowing with books. Once she was within reach, she grabbed the first thing that caught her attention, a brown leather journal similar to the one she remembered Logic writing in millions of times before at Intrigued.

Once it was in her hand, she found her way to the bed. She turned it in her hands, admiring it before she thumbed through it, found a random page and then opened it. Her eyes roamed the page, bringing a smile to her face. She scanned the words, feeling each one as if it were meant just for her eyes.

She continued moving through the pages until she stopped at a section that stood out to her. Reading the words felt familiar and intimate. She knew that the piece was about her. She read each word but certain ones stuck out: lustful stare, angelic face, kissable lips. He was writing about the things he wanted to do to her, to her body. It made Joy blush while also filling her with the sensations that she was somehow closer to him by reading his intimate thoughts about her.

She was so caught up in his words that she hadn't noticed that he was leaning against his doorframe, arms folded, watching her. A smirk adorned his face as he admired the intimacy of how his words affected her. Had she been anyone else, he would have felt slighted at his private thoughts being pillaged, but they were about Joy and he felt like they belonged to her, just as much as they belonged to him.

"That's personal," Logic said snatching Joy's attention away from his journal, so that she focused on him.

"I'm sorry, I didn't mean to—"

Logic chuckled as he entered his room and sat down next to her. "It's cool. I don't mind."

He smiled when he noticed how she blushed at his approval. "Are these about me?"

she asked looking from the journal into his dark brown eyes.

"A lot of them are," he said reaching for the journal, sliding it out of her small hands.

"How come you never performed these?" Joy asked.

"They were just for me. It allowed me to feel like I had something with you that no one else had," Logic admitted truthfully. "Come on, let's eat."

He stood, placing the journal on his dresser before reaching for Joy's hands. Once she was on her feet, she was held in his embrace, while his lips connected with hers.

"I missed you today," he confessed, before he led her back to the kitchen.

"You did?" Joy asked.

Logic laughed. "I think the proper response is, I missed you too Logic, but yes, I did."

Joy leaned against the counter and watched, as Logic removed two plates from the cabinet and then set them next to the food she brought with her. "You already know I missed you so I shouldn't have to say it."

He looked at her and smiled. Joy's eyes traced his body, which was covered in a pair of black jeans that housed a slight sag as they hung low around his waist, and a black pocket tee, which exposed his muscular arms that were covered with strategically placed tattoos. She followed his arms up to his shoulders and then his neck which displayed a few more tattoos, one of which was his brother's name and years of life.

Logic grabbed his jeans by the waist and tugged them just a little until they moved up his narrow waist, and then fell low around it again as if he had never even touched them in the first place. It was a movement he did often and was sexy to Joy, although pointless, because the slight sag he had was consistent.

"You see something you like?" Logic asked as he loaded their plates with equal amounts of food. Joy ate just as much as he did, which amazed him every time he watched her do it. He was just happy that she wasn't the type to shy away from food for appearance sake.

"I see a lot I like," Joy answered with a smug grin.

"Well I'll be sure to address that later. Grab some drinks and let's eat," Logic said over his shoulder, as he left the kitchen and made his way to the living room. Joy was right behind him carrying a beer for him and a bottle of water for herself.

"Tell me about your day," Logic said just before stuffing his mouth.

Joy chuckled and then glanced at him holding a fork full of food. "You don't want to hear about my kids."

"Yes I do, I bet you have a lot of stories to tell about those little bad asses." A smirk formed on Logic's face as he waited for Joy's reaction.

"Stop saying that, I told you my kids aren't bad."

He laughed. "Yeah aight, I bet they do shit like lock each other in the bathroom and tie shoe strings together and shit. I know they're bad. I don't know why you're fronting."

"You should come visit. You can be a guest speaker," Joy said grinning at him.

"Hell no. The fuck I look like chilling with a bunch of damn kids and what the hell would I talk to them about, selling dope?" Logic laughed at the idea.

"You're more than just that," Joy said and frowned, even though she knew he was only joking.

"Shit Joy, I know that, but I don't think that's a good fit for me," he said seriously.

"You're good with your nephew, I think you would do fine. You can come color with them." Joy offered up a playful smile.

"Nah, I'll let you have that. I'm good with Trent because it's part time and I'm just used to him. I don't fuck with kids too tough."

"What about your own?" Joy threw Logic with that statement, and he almost choked on his beer.

"The fuck you mean my own, I don't have no damn kids Joy."

The look on his face was so serious that Joy burst out laughing. "I know that. I mean if you ever have kids of your own."

Logic relaxed a little and set his half empty plate on the coffee table, before he took Joy's from her hands and placed it next to his. After that, he pulled her into his lap so that her legs her spewed across his and her side was pressed against his chest.

"You want to have my baby Joy?" Logic asked in a cocky tone.

"That is not what I meant," Joy returned just before he kissed her lips, sucking gently on her bottom one and then releasing it.

"I didn't say that was what you meant, but I'm asking you if you want to have my baby."

"One day, maybe." Joy could see a future with Logic and that future included a child, but for now she just wanted to enjoy the two of them.

He laughed and then kissed her again, this time a little deeper with more passion. "I'm not saying tomorrow Joy, just one day."

"Then yes."

"Good, because you didn't really have a say in that shit anyway."

Now Joy laughed. "I don't think it works like that but okay."

"Trust me, it works like that." Logic displayed a cocky grin after releasing his statement confidently.

"Hmm, I guess we'll see won't we."

*****

Logic lay next to Joy watching her sleep. He was on his side, propped up on his elbow with his head resting on a closed fist. His free hand glided down her cheek and occasionally through her hair. She was so beautiful to him and the more he lay there watching her, the more he fell under her spell. His emotions were tugging at the deepest part of his heart, because things were so complicated now. His life was complicated, which meant that her connection to him would surely make things difficult for her as well.

Rah kept creeping into his head, along with the murderous thoughts that flooded his mind about getting rid of him. Knowing that Rah once lay with Joy and had experienced what Logic was now claiming as his, infuriated him. Just that thought alone made him want to put a bullet in Rah's head. Adding in the fact that Rah wanted his territory, only made it worse.

Logic's intentions for the evening had originally been to question Joy about Rah, but the moment he was near her, he lost interest in hearing more about anything she had with Rah. He got caught up in just being with her and consumed by the idea of being inside her. Logic decided to save that for another day. For now, he just wanted to feel close to Joy. She calmed him in a way that no one else could and eased the tension of what he knew was to come: the war that was about to begin with Rah.

Logic's phone ripped him from his sleep and he jumped at the sound of it vibrating next to his head, but within seconds of it going off, he had it in his hand and to his ear.

"I need you to get here. We have a problem." Gotti's voice was serious and firm, so Logic immediately knew that something had to be up. He knew better than to question him over the phone, so instead he answered with, "I'm on my way."

He ended the call and looked down at Joy whose eyes were on him. This was the part that he didn't like; climbing out of bed in the middle of the night, to go deal with shit that only he was authorized to handle. Gotti and Lil Chris were well trained, and could do just about anything when it came to their business, but there were certain situations that needed Logic's approval before they were handled. Logic knew it came with the territory, and if he weren't having to leave in the middle of the night while Joy was in his bed, it wouldn't have bothered him so much.

"You're leaving?" Joy's voice was soft, but he could still hear the disappointment, so he moved towards her bringing his lips to hers.

"If I didn't have to go I wouldn't."

"It's fine, just be careful." This life wasn't new to Joy. She had experienced many nights where Rah left her alone in his bed or hers, to go handle business or somebody.

"Hopefully I won't be long." Again, Logic's lips found Joy's. She was making this hard for him. This was the first time he ever second guessed his decision to take care of business, and never once did Myesha have that effect on him. It was always business first, but with Joy he found himself having a mental war about whether or not he could actually leave.

Dressed in black jeans, a black hoodie and Timbs, gun strapped to his waist, Logic watched Joy who had drifted back to sleep. She was changing him and in ways that he wasn't ready to handle. He turned to leave, trying to shut her out of his mind because he needed to have his head right before he hit the streets. Logic had no idea what he was about to walk into, and Joy consuming his thoughts was definitely not a good look. As his door shut and he turned the key to lock it, he left everything he was feeling about Joy right there in his apartment and transformed into the Logic that had nothing to lose. That mindset was the only thing that would keep him safe.

-6-

The second Logic hit the last step to enter the basement, he knew something wasn't right. Gotti and Lil Chris had mugs on their faces and the few other members of his team that were in there with Gotti and Chris, looked like they were ready for battle.

"That's my damn brother Logic, what the fuck we gone do? How the hell am I supposed to go home and face my moms knowing that Marlo is in the fucking hospital barely breathing?"

Zeeno was standing inches away from Logic clenching his gun, which was at his side. Logic eyed it, but knew that no matter what had gone down, Zeeno wasn't about to use it on him. So he ignored his soldier who was standing in front of him and made eye contact with Gotti, looking for and explanation about what had everyone so fucked up.

"Rah's people hit our spot. They beat Marlo and left him for dead. Pulled him in the alley back behind Carter's. I think they set him up because he knows better than to make moves alone, but they got him good Logic. They don't know if he's gonna make it."

"He's gonna fucking make it," Zeeno said with a confidence that only a brother could have.

"Let's take a ride," Logic said looking right at Zeeno.

"You need me to go?" Gotti asked.

"Nah, you're good. Handle shit around here. Make sure our people know to be on the lookout. This won't happen again."

Gotti had been given his command. He nodded and watched as Zeeno and Logic left the basement. Logic led, with Zeeno right behind him. The two men walked to Logic's car, got in, and Logic pulled off.

The ride through College Park was quiet. Logic was in his head the entire time. He had been right where Zeeno was just a few months ago, with his brother Bernard, but the difference was that back then when shit went down, Logic knew his brother wasn't going to make it, while Zeeno was praying that his did.

They parked a few blocks away from where Rah's team usually worked and after his car was off, Logic looked Zeeno right in the eyes. "Pick one, any one you want."

Logic raised his hand and pointed towards his windshield down the block and two men he knew worked for Rah.

"I don't know who it was." Zeeno looked up confused but Logic spoke again.

"Doesn't matter, we'll take them all out one by one, until we get the right one, if that's what you need. I don't give a fuck. You mess with my people and you mess with me. We're team, so you asked me what the fuck we're gonna do, well this is what we're gonna do."

Logic meant every word he said. There was no hesitation whatsoever. Rah started a war and he was damn sure not going to back away from it.

Zeeno's eyes followed the men as they moved around clueless to the fact that their lives were hanging in the wind.

"I'll do whatever you need me to do to make this right. When I said we're family, I meant that shit so you tell me what you need."

"Take me to the hospital," Zeeno finally spoke up. The urge to kill, to get revenge was pulsing through his body, but his need for his brother to be okay was that much stronger. Right now, all he wanted was to check on his brother and make sure he was good.

Logic started his car and then looked at his soldier. "Whoever did that shit will pay. I promise you that. I'm giving you my word."

Zeeno nodded and Logic pulled off, en route to the hospital so that Zeeno could sit with his brother. Logic went in for a minute and eyed his badly beaten body. Marlo's face was black and blue, swollen and eyes shut tight. He had several broken bones in his face and body from where they stomped him after they beat him. It was hard to look at. Unlike Donte, Logic felt a sense of responsibility for all of his people, and to see Marlo lying there fighting for his life hit him hard. Logic wasn't soft by any means and he knew that this came with the territory, but it still hit him hard every time he had to witness it.

After speaking with the family and promising Zeeno that he would cover any expenses that they needed, Logic left. Before long, he was back on his block sitting in his car. His mind was working a lightning speed trying to figure out his next move. It wasn't as simple as just walking up to Rah and shooting him. He knew that, but this war Rah started was only the beginning. This was the part he didn't like. There was always somebody somewhere that felt like they could try you, take your shit and run it better than you. Logic had plans to handle anyone who tried, and Rah would be first.

Logic was so wrapped up in his head that he didn't see Gotti approach his car until he tapped the passenger side window. Logic pointed to it signaling for him to get in, which he did.

"What now? We can't let that shit slide Logic."

"We're not, trust me. We also can't be reckless. That's what he wants. If we react without thinking, then we'll make mistakes. We can't afford mistakes. I'm responsible for these guys, so when shit like this happens, I take it personal."

Gotti let Logic's words sink in for a minute before he spoke. "Sleep on it. We'll talk tomorrow. Go home, I got this shit for tonight."

Logic knew that there wasn't really anything he could do, but he felt it necessary to be around. As much as he wanted to go home and wrap his body around Joy's, he had to show support for his team. They needed him right now. His presence spoke more than any words he could offer them. If he respected them enough to be shoulder to shoulder with them, then they would trust him enough to follow his lead when the time was right.

"Nah, I'm gonna chill here for a minute," was all that Logic offered up before he opened his door to get out. Gotti didn't need an explanation. Logic's actions spoke for themselves so he nodded and let it go.

*****

Joy was fully dressed and finishing her hair when Logic finally walked through the door that morning. It was just after six and the second she laid eyes on him, she knew that he was tired and even more than that, she could see the stress radiating from his body. He smiled when she rounded the corner after hearing him enter his apartment, shutting the door behind him, but she could still see his worries hidden behind his smile. His mind was heavy and she wanted desperately to fix that for him.

After approaching him and sliding her arms around his neck, she pressed her lips against his, while his hands moved up her back. He pulled her into his body and returned a kiss that was a little deeper than the one she offered up. Her presence eased his mind a little and he couldn't help but connect it to the idea of this situation being a constant in his life.

"Damn you smell good. Why the hell you need to smell like fruit and shit just to go spend your day with those little bad ass kids?" Logic wore a devilish grin as he pulled back from Joy just enough to look into her eyes. Business was business and right now, he didn't want to bring that into what he and Joy had.

"You're gonna stop calling my kids bad and maybe I wanted to smell good for you." Joy offered up a smirk of her own before blessing him with another kiss, while attempting to pull his body closer to hers.

"Oh yeah?"

"Yeah." Joy released her hold on Logic and turned to head towards his bedroom. He followed close behind, watching her knee-length skirt cling nicely to her ass. He was currently processing the idea of sliding in her prior to her leaving for work.

Once they both reached his bedroom, Logic began removing his clothes while Joy added the finishing touches to hers. She watched him through the mirror on his dresser, as he removed his layers exposing his nicely toned body. The smile she plastered all over her face expressed approval. Logic moved behind her, his body fully exposed with the exception of the navy boxer briefs that he wore. His arms snaked around her waist while pressing his body firmly against hers.

"Keep that shit up and you'll be calling in." Logic spoke into her neck before kissing it.

Joy just laughed. "Keep what up?"

"Smiling at me like you see something you like while you're looking and smelling like this." Logic kissed Joy's neck multiple times before she pulled away. She knew that if he kept up that behavior she surely wouldn't be able to leave.

He just chuckled as he collected the clothes that he had just removed and tossed them into his hamper.

"I have to go. Are we doing something later?"

"We can, if that's what you want."

"Maybe." Joy didn't want to seem too eager but in all honesty, she would be content spending every free second she had with him.

"Call me when you get off." Logic moved past Joy, and kissed her on the cheek before leaving his room. She grabbed her purse and keys, purposely leaving her bags. Her plan was to return later so there was no point in collecting her things.

Once she hit the tiny hallway just outside Logic's room, she found him in his linen closet grabbing a towel and washcloth so that he could shower. He turned when he felt Joy near him.

"You change your mind?" Logic's expression was inviting, and Joy eyed his body while biting her bottom lip momentarily and then releasing it.

"Bye, I'll call you later." She stepped towards him stealing one last kiss and then left, before she changed her mind. Logic's presence was addictive to her and she was falling deeper and deeper with every second he was in her life.

-7-

Logic spent the day catching up on rest he missed from the night before. With everything going on he just needed a break. He planned on taking Joy out so that just the two of them could chill and forget about everything going on in their lives. Even if it was just for one night, he wanted to let go of everything and have Joy all to himself.

Once he was finally up and functional, he moved around his apartment doing various things. His first stop was the kitchen, for a quick breakfast of eggs and bacon. It was after one, but it was the easiest thing for him to make and he didn't feel like heading out. After he ate and cleaned up after himself, he decided to dress since he had taking a shower earlier after Joy left for work. Looking around his room he couldn't help but notice signs of Joy's presence in his life. She had body sprays and lotions on his dresser, clothes in his hamper and a toothbrush, body wash and hair supplies in his bathroom. Subtle things that made a huge statement, but he didn't mind; in fact, he was good with that.

After getting his room in order, Logic decided to chill for a while because he knew he had a few hours before Joy would be off work. He called and checked in with Gotti, to make sure everything was good on that end and after receiving confirmation that things were running smoothly, he got comfortable in his living room, armed with his remote. Even though he slept most of the morning, Logic still found himself drifting, that was until he heard someone at his door. Because only a handful of people knew where he lived and he never had company, his first move was to get his gun from the safe in his bedroom and secure it in the waist of his jeans. Once he reached his door, whoever was on the other side was impatiently banging on it, which struck a nerve with him, until he yelled through it and heard his mother's voice on the other side.

"What are you doing here?" Logic stepped aside to let his mother enter, and once she was inside and the door was shut and locked again, he kissed her on the cheek and waited for her to respond.

"I think we need to have a conversation." Mini looked at her son with a pained expression. She was conflicted about the fact that she knew he was in the streets again and she also knew that her opinion about it wasn't going to change it.

Logic motioned his hand towards his sofa and waited for his mother to take a seat before he did. Instead of sitting next to her, he positioned his body in front of her on the coffee table, while resting his elbows on his thighs and clasping his hands together. His eyes were locked on his mother as he waited.

"Why now?" she asked, holding a concerned gaze with her son.

"I can't answer that. It just needed to be done." Logic wasn't about to explain to his mother that he killed two men and had to either take over, or watch someone else run what he worked so hard to build.

"You think I don't know? I know about Donte and Fez. I know that you did it, what I don't understand is why now? This got something to do with that girl?"

"No, and don't go getting that idea in your head. She didn't want this for me any more than you did." Logic knew that was coming. He didn't want his family to blame Joy for a decision he made.

"Yeah, well it doesn't look that way."

"She don't have shit to do with it Ma. You wanna blame somebody, blame Najah for fucking with Fez when I told her to leave that nigga alone. Did you really think I was gonna let him put his hands on her and not do something about it? But even after all that, I made the decision; not Joy, not Najah, just me. I know you don't like it, and I know you're afraid for me but this is who I am, Ma. You just gotta accept that."

"So I should be okay with the fact that every time you walk out that door, you might not return? I'm a mother Auggie, your mother. I lost one son already, how do you expect me to accept that?"

Logic felt bad, he knew that his mother's heart was breaking but it wasn't going to change anything. The decision was made and there was no going back on that. This situation might not be forever, but it was his reality right now and there wasn't anything that he could do about it.

"You know I love you but I can't live for you," Logic said truthfully.

"I don't want you to live for me Augustus, I just want you to live. You're not a parent so I know that you don't understand that, but no parent wants to bury their child. Maybe that's selfish of me but I did that one time already and that haunts me everyday, I can't do that again."

Logic could see the persistence in his mother's request, but it wasn't going to change the situation. At this point, all he could do was give her the words she needed to hear, in hopes that she believed the sincerity and confidence behind them.

"I'm not going anywhere Ma. I promise you that."

"You can't make that promise, Augustus."

Logic realized that they were not going to see eye to eye on the matter, so he changed the subject. They discussed his nephew and sister, after which, moving to the topic of her and Luther. He watched his mother blush as she discussed what she attempted to pass off as a friendship, which Logic teased her about, knowing that they were far more than just friends. He talked with his mother until she had to leave to handle payroll for her employees, and then commenced to his original plan of relaxing until he heard for Joy. As much as he didn't want his mother to worry, he discerned that it was inevitable regardless of his feelings on the matter, so he made peace with that. He just prayed that she would be able to do the same.

*****

"Are you going to tell me where we're going?" Joy asked as she unzipped her skirt and let it fall to the floor. Logic traced her body contemplating the idea of the two of them staying in, as he watched Joy undress.

"Nope, it's a surprise. Just get dressed so that we can go."

Joy kneeled down to dig through her bag to retrieve a pair of jeans and Logic had to adjust himself as his body began to react to watching Joy from the position she was in. When she was standing again and stepping into her jeans, her face revealed her disapproval at the idea of Logic holding all the cards for their evening plans.

"Why won't you just tell me?" Joy's face turned into a slight pout as she zipped and buttoned her jeans. After she was done, she stood firmly in front of Logic with her arms folded as her face contorted into a scowl, hoping that Logic would give into her demand.

"You're not five so that shit won't work." Logic pointed at Joy's face, released a cocky grin and then walked to his closet so that he could finish dressing.

"I might as well be; you're treating me like I am since you won't tell me where we're going." Joy mumbled as she pulled her shirt over her head.

Logic stepped out of the closet with a pair of Nikes in his hand, and kissed Joy on the neck before he positioned himself on the bed to put them on.

"So because I want to surprise you, I'm treating you like you're five?" Logic asked without making eye contact with Joy because he was putting his shoes on, while she was collecting the clothes that she had just removed and dumping them into his hamper. He smiled watching her move around his bedroom, like she was claiming it as her own.

Joy laughed, realizing how crazy she sounded, but she didn't care, she just wanted him to tell her where they were going. She was impatient and it was driving her crazy not knowing.

"Yes, so just tell me." She watched as Logic stood, adjusted his jeans which fell right back into place, before her arms slid around his waist and she looked up at him.

"No, you'll see when we get there so you can chill with the sucking up ma. I'm not going to tell you."

He kissed her before he let her go and a smirk formed on his face. "Now hurry and you can find out."

"You make me sick." Joy rolled her eyes and left the room so that she could head to the bathroom to fix her hair.

Once they were done preparing to leave, she handed Logic the keys to her car. He opened the passenger side door for her and then got into the driver side. Shortly after they were on the road, going God knows where, Joy filled him in on her day. Joy rambled on about her kids, and he admired how passionately she talked about them. You would think that she was personally invested in every single one of them the way she carried on about them. He loved that about her.

An hour later, after a quick stop at a grocery store for dinner and a few supplies, they arrived at Lake Lanier, where Logic owned a lake house which he originally purchased for his mother. They used to go as a family, but it had been awhile. After he got out the game, it was one of the few things he actually decided to keep, but it had been awhile since any of this family members had been there.

"Who's house is this?" Joy asked looking around as they both got out and began collecting the groceries they stopped and purchased.

"Mine," he answered nonchalantly.

Joy stopped dead in her tracks and stared at him. "Yours...why do you have a lake house?"

He chuckled. "Does that really matter?" he asked, as he used his body to shut her back door, and then waited for Joy to join him so that they could head towards the house.

"Yeah, it kind of does. It doesn't really seem like your thing," Joy answered truthfully.

Logic laughed and then looked back across his shoulder in Joy's direction. Once they reached the front porch, he waited for Joy to join him before instructing her to get his keys out of his pocket. She lingered a little longer than she needed to, which made him smile.

"What's my thing?" Logic asked after they were inside and had the groceries on the counter in the kitchen. He was moving around the living room and kitchen turning on lights while Joy admired the beauty of the place. It was simple but nice, and gave you a sort of cozy feel. She instantly fell in love with it.

She laughed realizing how it must have sounded. "I don't know, not this. It's too domestic."

"Damn Joy. I told you I'm more than just a street nigga, but you right though. I bought this shit for my mom. She wanted a vacation home. I just wanted to buy her a house to live in, but she refused to move and instead, this is what she wanted. A place for us to escape reality as she put it. Some perfect family type shit. I guess it made her feel like life was more than just me and Nard running the streets and Najah fucking around with dope boys. Out here, we were just us."

"So what's lakehouse Logic like?" Joy asked, eyeing Logic with a grin as he leaned against the counter in the kitchen. He looked so sexy to her as she traced the contours of his body.

"Don't shit about me change," he said and then winked at her.

"Yeah, I bet," Joy said and then grinned. "I hope I'm not just being added to the list of females that you bring here," Joy said as she made her way over to him, leaning into his body.

He chuckled at the idea of her being jealous or feeling like she was just anybody. "Aside from my moms, Nova and Najah, you're the only other woman who's ever been here. So chill with all that jealous shit."

"I'm not jealous, just curious."

"Yeah aight." Logic pulled Joy further into his body before he kissed her again and then let her go.

"We didn't bring anything with us," Joy said as she began taking their groceries out of the bags.

"Anything like what?"

"Are we not staying?" she asked.

"Nah, just dinner and then we can chill for a while. You know you have to go deal with them bad ass kids tomorrow and I have some shit I need to do, but we can come up here one weekend and stay."

"This weekend?" Joy asked with a childlike grin.

"No, but soon. I just wanted one night with you, no interruptions."

"I guess I can live with that," Joy said which made him laugh.

"I promise; I'll make it worth your while." Logic moved behind Joy, pressing his body against hers so that she was clear about his plans for the two of them.

About an hour later, they were sitting on the floor in the living room finishing the dinner that they prepared together, or rather Joy prepared while Logic watched. Joy had come out of her jeans and was currently in just her shirt and a pair of lace panties, while Logic only had on his jeans. He was waiting with his back against the sofa while Joy was across from him, sitting Indian Style with her plate centered between her legs.

The two were deep in conversation about random things like their childhoods, Joy's dysfunctional parents and the fact that Logic knew very little about his dad. He didn't seem to care much about that, because as far as he was concerned, Luther had been the man in his life.

Joy lifted her plate and set it on the floor next to her before she crawled over and positioned herself on Logic's lap. His hands gripped her butt and then moved under her shirt up her back, while their gazes were locked on each other.

"You make shit easy, you know that?" Logic admitted, not really knowing where the thought came from.

"What's that supposed to mean?"

"When I'm with you, like this, I don't have to think. Shit just flows and I need that. Sometimes life can be so complicated that the simplest things mean the most."

Joy smiled at his confession. He was always so confident and sure of everything, but him telling her that was like him admitting a weakness, like she somehow gave him a strength that he didn't have.

"I'm glad that I can be that for you." Joy leaned in and placed her lips against his before she continued. "I'll be whatever you need me to be," she whispered against his lips, before transitioning into a kiss. She meant that too. At this point, all that mattered was that they had each other. Nothing else matter and as far as she was concerned, that was the way it was going to always be.

-8-

Logic pulled up on the block, looking around at his people working in the background. Things seemed calm which was a good thing. He and Joy had gotten in late last night, but it was worth it to be able to spend time with her and forget about everything else he was dealing with. Now, it was back to business. Logic and Gotti had a meeting with their supplier to renegotiate their deal. Product was moving, so Logic wanted to increase what he was getting but only if they could get better pricing. If not, he planned on finding another source. After Gotti left instructions with Lil Chris about how to handle things, he got in the car with Logic to roll out.

"Yo, what up Logic? We ready for this shit?"

Logic nodded as he pulled off en route to the restaurant where they were going to meet Soloman. Logic didn't trust back alley deals, so he always made sure his meetings were set up in public places, less chance of someone doing some dumb shit. He was always thinking ahead.

"We're making money, Logic, why won't you get rid of this shit?" Gotti asked looking around Logic's car.

He cut his eyes at Gotti and then focused on the road. "Flashy shit brings attention. I don't really give a fuck about things and I damn sure don't want or need the attention. I'm good on that."

Gotti chuckled. He knew Logic well. Even when they had money rolling in on the regular, Logic still lived modestly. He once had a downtown apartment which was nice, but nothing over the top. Even when Logic's bank accounts were filled with commas, no one would have been able to tell. It wasn't really his thing.

In fact, the lake house he purchased was the most expensive thing he ever owned. The house his mother lived in was one of Luther's properties, that she eventually purchased from him and refused to leave, even after Logic offered to have a house built for her. Mini said she never wanted a big ass house that could be snatched away from her at anytime, so she stayed put and Logic purchased the lake house as her escape.

"Nothing's wrong with a splurge every once in awhile, but I feel you though. So what's the deal. If Soloman doesn't budge, then we going somewhere else?"

"Depends. We need good shit but at good prices. Quality hasn't been an issue so, I don't wanna fuck with that," Logic answered truthfully.

"True, and so far, we're not getting any complaints."

"I wanna keep it that way."

"What's the deal with Rah? He's been quiet since his people went in on Marlo. You heard anything?"

"Nah, he knows we're on alert right now, so I know he's gonna lay back for a minute. He was probably expecting us to hit hard after fucking with our team, which is why we didn't. I'm sure it's fucking with him because he doesn't know what to expect. Donte was reckless and did dumb shit, so right now he's trying to figure out our next move.

Logic was more or less working the plan out in his head as he spoke to Gotti. He liked to process things before he reacted. It made it hard for people to catch them off guard if he had things thought out.

"So what is our next move?" Gotti asked.

Logic chuckled. He wanted to put a bullet in Rah's head. More so because of his history with Joy, but also because Rah was stupid enough to fuck with his people.

"We get rid of the problem and expand."

After offering up an arrogant grin, Gotti nodded and the two rode in silence the rest of the way to meet Soloman.

"Logic, it's been awhile. I can't say that I'm disappointed to see you though. Dealing with Donte was mentally taxing." Soloman offered a confident smile as he stood and extended a hand which Logic accepted and then Soloman addressed Gotti.

"Are you happy to have your leader back? I'm sure working under Donte made things a bit complicated for your team."

Gotti nodded but didn't speak as the three men sat down at our corner table. Logic looked around the restaurant and realizing that he and Gotti stood out. Soloman was dressed in suit pants and a button up shirt, no jacket or tie but still business like, while Gotti and Logic were both dressed down in jeans and Timbs. Logic was rocking a burgundy Henley while Gotti was dressed in a plain front black sweatshirt, his usual attire. The people around them were dressed similar to Soloman, if not more professional, but Logic didn't really give a fuck. Status didn't affect him. Money or not, his confidence was through the roof and he always carried himself that way. Clothes didn't make the man, his confidence did, and Logic had enough to rock with the best of them.

Logic leaned back in his chair, propping his elbows up on the arms, while studying Soloman face. He returned the favor as if trying to read Logic, while Gotti's eyes moved back and forth between the two men. Gotti understood his role in this meeting, so he kept quiet and waited.

"So, I understand you want to increase your supplies?"

"Things are good right now so why not?" Logic released casually. He didn't offer up any indication as to what his mood was, making him hard for Soloman to read.

"How much of an increase?"

"Depends on what you're offering. The deal that Donte had set up with you is bullshit. You know it and I know it. I want good shit, but I'm not going to break the bank to get it. You give me your best offer and I'll let you know whether or not I'm going to find a new supplier. I don't give a shit about relationships. If you're not willing to give me what I need then I'm sure I can find someone who is."

Gotti was a little taken aback by the cocky way that Logic addressed Soloman. Logic had always been that way, so Gotti wasn't surprised, but seeing him in action, having a front row seat to him taking charge and making demands, gave him a rush.

Soloman chuckled. "This is why I like you. You say what you want and you don't accept anything less than that. Donte was a pussy, a joke. He didn't know shit about business. You, on the other hand, handle yourself like a man in charge. I like that."

"All due respect Soloman, your opinion of me don't make my dick hard. I'm here to talk numbers."

"Understood." Soloman nodded and laid out what he was willing to offer, and Logic returned what he was willing to accept. An hour later, the two men had reached an agreement and had a date set up for their next drop. Gotti was to pick up and deliver the money a week from today.

"You know he don't like your ass for handling him like that?" Gotti said with a grin as Logic made his way back across town.

Logic chuckled. "I don't give a fuck. Business is business. You either want my money or you don't, but fuck all that bowing down, song and dance shit. I don't need it. He don't have to like me to do business with me." Logic found himself falling back into his role easily. He had always been confident. There was always a way to get what you needed, so he would never kiss ass, no matter how important someone thought they were.

"I feel you, but that shit was still funny as hell yo. He wanted to check you but he knew better."

Logic shook his head and pulled out his ringing phone. The thought of Soloman trying to check him made him laugh. He always had one in the chamber for anyone who thought they were man enough to challenge him.

"What's up Nah Nah?"

"I need a huge favor. I have a test and Trent's school just called. He's sick and needs someone to come get him now. I can't find Mommy, she won't answer my calls, and Nova's at work. Will you get him for me? I should be done with my test in an hour and then I can meet you at Mommy's house."

Logic looked across at Gotti. He was near his nephew's school and didn't want to drive all the way to the block to drop Gotti off, and they still had a few things to discuss.

"Yeah, I got you. Just hurry up Najah, I have shit to do."

"I will, I'm sorry, but this is a midterm and I can't miss it. Thanks Auggie. I'll be there as soon as I can, and I already called the school so they know you're coming."

"How the fuck you already called them but you didn't know if I was going to agree?" Logic snapped playfully.

"'Cause, I know you always got me. Love you Auggie. I gotta go."

Najah hung up so that Logic wouldn't have a chance to respond. Again, he shook his head and placed his phone into his cup holder. Gotti now had his eyes on him trying to figure out what was going on.

"Yo, I need to go pick up my nephew and take him to my mom's crib to wait for my sister. You want me to take you back or can you chill for a minute? We need to map out how to divide up this increase that we're getting next week."

"Shit, I'm good. I'll check in with Lil Chris to make sure he don't need me though."

Logic nodded and changed directions so that he could head to Trent's school. Once they arrived, Gotti stayed in the car and called Lil Chris while Logic got out to get his nephew.

After the office buzzed him in, he made his way to it and was hit with lustful eyes and grins from the two women that worked in the office. He could tell from the way they were eye fucking him, that they wanted to offer up more than his nephew. This was the norm every time he showed up to pick Trent up.

"Can I help you?" one of them asked leaning across the counter, putting her double D's on display. Logic laughed under his breath at how inappropriately she was dressed to be working at an elementary school. He wished Joy would pull some shit like that.

"I need to get my nephew, Trent Ford."

"And you are?" the other woman asked, offering up a big ass seductive grin that made her home girl roll her eyes.

"Logic Ford," Logic answered, knowing good and damn well that she knew who he was. He had been there to get Trent plenty of times before.

"You sure he's your nephew and not your son? He looks just like you, with his adorable self," she added.

Logic chuckled because he knew that she was just talking. Trent was a duplicate of his bitch ass father. "I don't have any kids, ma. That, I'm sure of."

"That's hard to believe, with your fine ass," she mumbled as she began typing something into her computer.

"Do you have ID?" she asked.

Logic pulled out his wallet and held up his license, making sure to cover his address with his fingers. She reached for it, but he held it out so that she could see it without having to actually hold it. She was a little too aggressive and the last thing he wanted was a surprise visit at his apartment. The other woman laughed.

"Thank you Augustus," she snapped, annoyed by the fact that she knew he didn't want her to get his information.

"Cynthia, can you get Trent please?"

Now she was rolling her eyes, because she didn't want to leave Logic alone with her home girl, like it was going to somehow make her miss out on the chance to get with him, but he wasn't interested in either one of them.

A few minutes later, Trent came walking around the corner from the back of the office. Old girl was rubbing his shoulders and Trent looked irritated. He pulled away from her and walked right up to Logic and leaned against him. Logic reached for Trent's book bag, tossed it over his shoulder and then looked at the two women.

"We good or you need anything else?"

"No, you're good. Trent, I hope you feel better baby. We're going to miss you for the rest of the day."

Trent scrunched up his face, but didn't say anything, and Logic laughed at his nephew. Even at six years old, he didn't really give a fuck about much, a trait that he likely picked up from him. Once they got in the car, Trent climbed in the backseat and leaned against the door.

Logic watched him from the rearview mirror as they pulled off.

"Trent, you know those women like that?" Logic asked knowing that they were only pining over his nephew because they wanted to get at him.

Trent looked up with a smirk. "Nope, but they want to know you. I heard them talking about it after Mommy called. They both said you could get it. They want the D." Logic had been to Trent's school multiple times before, so all the women in the office were familiar with him. He had never entertained any of their advances, but it was clear that he could have either one of them if he wanted.

Logic chuckled, not even bothering to check his nephew and Gotti turned to glance at Trent, who now had his eyes closed. "Damn it's like that, lil dude don't have no filters does he?" Logic laughed thinking about his nephew. Trent was a lot like him when it came to certain things.

Three hours later, Najah came busting through the door carrying a stack of books, which she dropped on the floor and started explaining why it took her so long.

"Before you even say anything, I tried to get here. My psych test was all essay questions and that shit took forever. I owe you Auggie. I already know." Najah was so caught up in explaining and removing her purse and jacket, that she hadn't realized that Gotti was in the room with them. He was on the sofa next to Trent in the middle of a game.

"Your ass always owes me Nah Nah," Logic said as he neared his sister to kiss her on the cheek.

"Yo, let's roll," Logic said addressing Gotti, which directed Najah's attention to him and she smiled, because he instantly caught her eye. Gotti was only about 5'9" but still taller than Najah, who was barely 5'2", being short like her mother. His mocha complexion was accented with dark round eyes, thick eyebrows and a low neatly trimmed beard, that he rubbed with his hand before it went across his short spiked dreads.

His eyes met Najah's and he offered up a partial smile.

"Aight yo, I'll catch you next time Trent." Gotti coarsely ran his head across Trent's head, before he held up a closed fist to give him dap and then stood. He moved past Najah, who couldn't help but take in his cologne as it swept her nose when he passed.

"Your shorty is a little beast on that 2K, but he still can't rock with me though," Gotti said to Najah and then turned to face Trent.

"I got you next time," Trent said not looking back because he was caught up in the game.

"Yeah, we'll see about that," Gotti said.

"Aight Nah Nah, we're out." Logic didn't bother introducing his sister to Gotti because he didn't want her getting any ideas about fucking around with anybody on his team. Gotti was good people but business needed to stay business.

"It was nice to meet you," Najah said not knowing what else to do to get his attention. She knew Logic, so him not introducing her to his homeboy was his way of saying that Gotti was off limits, but she was hard headed and intrigued by Gotti.

"Same here ma," was all he said before he offered a wink, and followed Logic to the door. He was also feeling Najah, but planned on feeling Logic out about her before he took it there, so he left it at that and without another word, the two men left.

-9-

"Where's Lan?" Joy asked as she got comfy on the sofa while Karma was in the kitchen getting them drinks and snacks. Since Joy and Logic had gotten together, the two had barely spent anytime together and they were overdue for some much needed girl time.

"In Chicago."

"Chicago, for work?"

Karma rolled her eyes. "Let him tell it, yeah. I really don't know what he does half the time, but it's cool though."

"Don't do that. You know Lan isn't checking for anybody but you, so just stop."

"I used to believe that, but lately he's been acting weird. I know he travels a lot but it's like every other week now and when I ask to go he's like, 'nah K, all you're gonna do is complain'."

Joy laughed. "And he's right. You hate being in the studio, you hate Lexus because you swear they're fucking, even though he has proven to you more times than I can even remember that they're not, and you know you can't just leave work like that. He's trying to make a name for himself, K. He loves music, so he has to get out there to push his beats or it will never happen for him."

Joy shook her head thinking about Karma and Landon. He was nice with his beats, it was like breathing to him, but he still hadn't quite found that one yet. Lexus was an artist that he was producing for, but she was still new and had just gotten her deal, so he was hoping that she would be his big break. They spent a lot of time together and Lexus clearly had a thing for him, but the first time she let it be known, Lan shut it down. He and Karma had been through so much, mostly because of his cheating but after one big fall out, a four-month separation and Lan seeing Karma with another guy, he realized that he needed to get his shit together. They had been tight ever since and as far as either of them knew, he was faithful. Aside from the fact that they argued all the time, things were good, and even with the arguing they were good. That was just their thing. It drove Joy crazy to be around them sometimes, but she knew they loved each other.

"He might not me messing with that hoe now, but it doesn't mean she's not trying. You know just like I know that she wants my man. I'll cut that hoe though so she better stay in her lane."

Joy burst out laughing which made Karma laugh, because she knew she sounded crazy but she didn't care. She wasn't letting go of Landon and especially not to Lexus."

"You," Joy pointed to Karma, "need to trust your man before you push him away, because your crazy ass got trust issues."

"I do trust him... kind of, but any issues I have are his fault, so he'd better just deal with it." Karma rolled her eyes.

"I'm not messing with you like that." Joy grabbed a few of the tortilla chips that Karma set between them and dipped one in her queso that was on the table.

"So what's up with you and your boy? Y'all good?"

Joy smiled at the mention of Logic. She couldn't help the feelings that surfaced because of him. "We're good. Just trying to find our rhythm. It's weird because everything I know about him is changing. He's such a different person now."

"Different how Joy?" Karma looked at Joy concerned. She had been through too much with Rah and Joy, and wasn't about to take that route again if Logic was turning into Rah.

Karma used to be a stripper and she had no shame in that, but because of the lifestyle, she had dealt with enough dope boys in her past to know that not many of them were faithful. Rah was a habitual cheater and he liked to use his hands when Joy called him on it.

Joy could read exactly what Karma was thinking, so she quickly cleared up any misconceptions that she might be processing about Logic. "He's not Rah, K. Nothing like him at all. He's just so confident now, like his true self is coming through." Joy was grinning as she thought about him. He had always seemed confident and cocky, but over the past few weeks, it had just gone to a whole other level.

Karma just stared at Joy for a moment as if trying to decide if she wanted to believe her best friend, before a grin started to creep through. "Somebody's feeling their new boo a little bit I see."

"Shut up." Now Joy really couldn't contain her smile.

"It's all good boo. Good dick will do it to you every time," Karma said with a smirk.

"See, why you always gotta take it there. This don't have anything to do with that. I just like him." Joy rolled her eyes, and what she was saying was partially true. She did genuinely like Logic, hell, how could she not. He was smart, sexy as hell, confident, arrogant and he handled her body like it was created just for him and him alone, but it wasn't just about the sex. He made her pulse race, her heart pound in her chest, and that feeling was addictive.

"Girl I'm just playing, but I'm glad you're happy. I just need him to do right by you and keep you safe. You were my bae long before you ever laid eyes on his sexy ass. So make sure he doesn't get that twisted," Karma said while meaning every word. Dope boys meant problems and she wasn't about to lose Joy to any nonsense, so if Logic couldn't keep her safe, then he needed to fall off.

Joy blew Karma a kiss. "You'll always be my bae, with or without him."

"Good, then he won't mind if you stay with me tonight. I don't wanna be in this house by myself and Lan won't be back until tomorrow."

Joy laughed. "Oh, so you're only professing your love because your scary ass don't want to stay in this house by yourself. That's foul K."

"Girl bye, you know I love you whether you stay or not, but that's what best friends are for. If you can't use them, then what are they good for." She picked up Joy's phone off the sofa and shoved it towards her. "Now call your man and tell him you're with me tonight." She offered up a sneaky grin. Joy grabbed her phone and rolled her eyes. Logic mentioned that he had things to do, so she hoped that he wouldn't mind her staying with Karma. Either way, it was a done deal so he would have to survive, but would she, was the real question.

*****

Logic was deep in his head, scribbling down his thoughts which were currently about Joy. He was sitting in his bedroom when he glanced at his dresser, noticing a cluster of her things. That led to thoughts about her and her smile, which eventually turned into visions of her naked body in his bed. The images were so vivid that he grabbed his journal and began jotting down what he was feeling. With everything going on, it had been a minute since his thoughts escaped the sanctuary of his mind and made it onto paper. Logic was so lost in what he was thinking, that he hadn't noticed his phone going off until its second notification, which caused him to look down at it. There was a text from Joy which flashed across the screen, forcing a smile to spread across his face face. That was until he read the message, that immediately caused him to call her instead of replying.

"Why you gotta stay all night? Just come home, even if it's late. I want you in my bed."

"Home?" Logic could hear the smile in Joy's voice as she teased him about his choice of words.

"You know what the fuck I mean, but yeah, home. Shit, I'm not gonna front, my bed is your bed and I want you in it."

"It's just one night. Lan's out of town and Karma wants me to stay."

Logic was feeling selfish as hell because he damn sure didn't want to share Joy, not even with her best friend, so he said what he knew he should say, even though he didn't mean one word of it.

"You're good, ma. I've had you wrapped up lately and I know you need that time with your girl. I've got some shit to do anyway."

"You sure?"

"Hell yeah, he's sure. Now hang up before he brings his ass over here to get you and I have to cut him too," Karma yelled in the background causing Logic to laugh.

"Yo, she's half right. Shoot me her address. I'm gonna swing by there in a little while, since you're not bringing your ass home tonight."

"You sure are real comfortable with that," Joy laughed at the fact that Logic said home again, in reference to her absence.

"Hell yeah I am, and you better be too," Logic said arrogantly.

"I'll get back to you on that," Joy teased. "What time are you coming?"

"Oh hell no. Didn't she just tell you that she's staying with me tonight?" Karma leaned towards Joy and yelled through the phone to make sure Logic could hear her.

"Put me on speaker," he said.

"No, I'm not doing that."

He chuckled. "Joy, put me on speaker."

"Fine."

She removed her phone from her face and put it on speaker.

"Yo, chill with all that. I'm not coming to get her, but I am coming to see her later. You can't just kidnap my girl and expect me to be okay with that Karma."

"Your ass needs to learn how to spend one night away from her, damn. She got you sprung like that?" Karma snapped.

"Hell yeah, she does, and I'll admit that shit too. Cut a nigga some slack." Logic was joking but there was truth behind it too. In just a short amount of time, he realized that Joy was his comfort zone, and that feeling was crucial to his sanity right now.

"Just don't try any slick shit like trying to talk her into leaving with you and we're good, but trust me, I'm setting a timer the second you hit my front porch. Hell, I might not even let your ass come in."

Joy bursted out laughing and so did Logic. Joy looked across at Karma because she knew that Karma was dead ass serious.

"Damn Karma, it's like that. You gonna set a timer and shit?" Logic asked.

"Yep, now play if you want, and I thought you had something to do. She's busy right now, so bye."

"K, stop playing," Joy yelled as Karma tried to snatch Joy's phone.

"Yo, I'm out. Send me the address and I'll see you in a few hours," Logic said.

"Bye Logic," Karma yelled.

After Joy ended the call, her index finger pointed straight at Karma. "You know you're wrong for that," Joy wore a smirk.

"What?" Karma asked pretending to not to have a clue about what Joy was talking about. She held a serious stare for all of ten seconds before a smile began to surface.

"That right there." Joy made a circle in the air, using her finger like she was outlining Karma's face.

"Girl bye. He has you all the time. I just want one night. You owe me that, especially since you wouldn't have been with him in the first place, if it wasn't for me."

Joy rolled her eyes. "You better be glad I love you and you have good snacks."

They both laughed this time and Joy lifted her phone to send Logic Karma's address. She was looking forward to seeing him later, even if Karma was going to have a timer running, but for now she was about to enjoy some much needed girl time. She had to admit, she missed her best friend and was glad that she was being held hostage.

-10-

Logic had free time on his hand and nothing to do with it, so after he ran through the block to make sure things were running smoothly, he decided to go check on his cousin. They hadn't talked since the day she showed up at his mother's house with Rah. He was still a little pissed about it, but he couldn't really blame her for some shit she didn't know. But he also needed it to be clear that she wasn't fucking with Rah on any type of level. After that, if she decided to do some dumb shit concerning Rah, Logic was going to have to check her. Being that he was the only man in either of their lives, he felt obligated to see that they were protected and made good choices which included the men they were involved with. He also understood that they were grown and could ultimately do what they wanted, but Rah was the one exception. Rah would die before Logic let Nova deal with him.

"You could have called first," Nova released sarcastically when Logic walked through her front door.

He just laughed and dropped his keys on her coffee table, and sat down on the love seat across from her.

"That key is for emergencies, not just so you can walk up in here invading my privacy whenever you feel like it," Nova continued to speak even though Logic didn't.

"You want you key back?" Logic leaned forward to reach for his keys but Nova just rolled her eyes, which made Logic chuckle. She and Najah were so much alike, both his cousin and his sister felt like they had all the answers but when it came to men, they couldn't pick the right one to save their lives.

"Why are you here Auggie? Clearly you care more about what your girl thinks than what I think." Nova was still a little put off by the fact that Logic defended Joy instead of her, even though she knew that Joy hadn't really done anything wrong. Her past with Rah wasn't relevant to the fact that Nova was dealing with him now.

"I'm here because we need to talk and don't pull that childish shit with me. You grown as fuck Nova, so don't come with that I hurt your feeling shit. You know you were wrong for coming at Joy like that anyway. If anything, she should have been in your ass since you were the one fucking with her leftovers, but as you can see, she didn't give a fuck about any of that. So get your feelings in check about that bullshit and let it go. That nigga is on borrowed time anyway, trust me."

Nova sat there fuming, mostly because Logic was right, but also because he mentioned handling Rah. She knew from the tension between Rah and Logic that something was going on that was bigger than the fact that Rah and Joy had history, but she also knew that that same history was a big motivator for Logic wanting to get rid of him.

"So you ready to kill for her. You just met the damn girl a few months ago Auggie." Nova stood, snatching up the plate and cup she had been using, so that she could head to the kitchen. Logic was right behind her.

"You sound real fucking childish right now. Would I kill that nigga because he used to fuck with Joy? Hell yeah if he didn't know his place, which clearly he doesn't since he disrespected your ass right there in front of everybody, but this shit isn't just about Joy. It's also about him fucking with my team and trying to take what's mine. You know me and you know that shit ain't gonna fly. No one is exempt and I got one chambered for any motherfucker that tries me. Just because you're fucking him don't give that nigga a pass. If anything it pushes him to the top of the fucking list. Family first always, and just because you got your damn feelings on your shoulder, don't change the fact that I'm always going to make sure you're good, even when you're too damn stubborn to see it."

Nova knew that Logic was right, but her pride was tugging at her and she was having a hard time admitting it.

Logic watched Nova moving around her kitchen slamming dishes and cabinets to make a point. He didn't really care. Growing up around his mom, Najah and Nova had him used to women being in their feelings. It didn't really move him one way or the other, and he was an expert at tuning it out. Logic was extremely intelligent, regardless of the fact that his formal education ended at age sixteen, so he processed every situation and dealt with the them in a way that always allowed him to control the outcome. He had a gift for forcing people to feed off of his energy, so he never just reacted. Every thought, every action for him was planned. Just like now, he allowed Nova her moment, knowing that when she realized that he wasn't moved by her temper tantrum, she would eventually calm down so that they could have a conversation that wasn't driven by her personal feelings.

"Where are Kenyan and Kenya?" Logic asked just now realizing that he hadn't seen or heard his cousins since he got there. Unless they were sleep, they would have been all over him.

"Sharece picked them up so that they could play at her house with for a while." This time Nova answered a little more relaxed. She didn't dare tell him that she sent her kids with Sharece because Rah was coming over.

Logic looked at her questionably. Nova was a good mother, the best in fact, because her kids' father wasn't shit so she had to be. It was just her, and that meant that she had them with her all the time. If she was home, they were home with her and when she wasn't, they were usually with Najah or his mom.

"You have to work?"

"No, they just wanted to go play so I told her it was cool. I'm getting them in a little while," Nova said hoping she didn't sound suspect.

"Aight, well you ready to talk like you got some damn sense or do we need to do this another time?"

Nova rolled her eyes before turning aggressively, folding her arms and leaning against the counter in front of her kitchen sink. Logic shook his head and stood in front of her.

"Look, I know you call yourself feeling that nigga but he's bad news Nova. After that bullshit that went down at Mom's house, I know you already know that. Is that really what you want, a nigga that don't really give a fuck about your feelings? You can't sit here and tell me that shit wasn't foul as hell."

"I'm not messing with him anymore, so it doesn't matter," Nova lied, while Logic studied her face. He knew his cousin.

"Yeah, aight. It's whatever. Like I said, you're grown but trust me, I don't make threats, I make promises and I promise that muthafucker won't be breathing for long. You can be slick and be on some disrespectful shit if you want to, but I'm telling you now, fuck your feelings for him and if you let him get you caught in the middle of a bad situation, then that's on you. You're my family and I always got you, but some shit I can't save you from."

"What's that supposed to mean?" Nova almost felt like Logic was threatening her.

"It means that the line is drawn, choose a side."

She stared at him for a minute, knowing what she she should say and honestly there wasn't really a choice to be made. She knew what side she was on but right now, she was going to find a way to have the best of both worlds. She just had to be careful. If nothing else, Nova knew that Logic was a man of his word and he didn't play when it came to family and loyalty, but what was the harm in it if it was understood that she wasn't going to get serious with Rah. That much she knew.

"There's no choice to be made Auggie, and I hope you know me better than that. I would never go against you or this family."

Now it was Logic's turn to process. He watched his cousin's face knowing damn well she was lying, but calling her on it wasn't going to change anything. He just hoped she understood the position she was putting herself in, the position she was putting him in. Rah was going to get her fucked up and he could feel it coming. He just prayed that it wasn't a situation that they couldn't recover from.

"I have to go. I'll catch up with you soon," was all that he said before he pulled Nova into a hug and kissed her on the forehead. She walked him to the door and just before he was about to leave she spoke again.

"I'll make it right with Joy," Nova said.

Logic just chuckled, nodded and then left.

*****

Rah smiled at Nova the second she opened her front door but she returned a nasty glare. *Here we fucking go with the bullshit.* He assumed it was because he hadn't been returning her calls but he didn't really care. He had been busy watching Logic's people and making plans. After a few of his guys put one of Logic's guys in the hospital, he thought for sure that Logic's team would come at him hard, but they hadn't made a move yet. Rah wasn't sure how to take that, so he had been on the streets with Moses and his people trying to figure out what they were up to. As far as they could tell, it was business as usual for Logic's team, but Rah was smart enough to know that things aren't always what they appeared. He had done his research on Logic, so he had a little inside information about how he made moves. He knew that Logic was a thinker, rarely ever did he just react, so Rah took that to mean that they were planning. It didn't matter to him because he was planning too. He was too arrogant to believe that anyone could take him down, and especially not some poetry writing, street imposter wannabe.

"You want me to leave?" Rah asked offering up a slick smile that he knew Nova wouldn't be able to resist. He could see her damn near drooling just from the fact that he actually showed up.

"What I want is to know why you're fucking with me. If this is about trying to get under my cousin's skin, then yeah, you can leave because trust me, that's the wrong move." Nova made sure to keep eye contact with Rah so that she could hopefully read his reaction. She really wanted him to be there, but if this was about Logic then she wasn't about play those games with Rah. Logic had already basically threatened her, and she wasn't about to prove him right by getting caught up in some situation where Rah was using her just to fuck with Logic.

Rah laughed and stepped past Nova inside her apartment, but slapping her hard on the side of her thigh before he was completely inside. She tilted her head back slightly, rolling her eyes to the ceiling while still holding her door, which she eventually shut after letting out a long frustrated breath. Like always, Rah went straight to her bedroom and when she entered, he was in the process of removing his clothes. Once he was down to just his jeans and nothing else, he sat on the foot of her bed with his eyes focused on her, as she leaned against her dresser watching him. Nova needed to keep some distance between the two or she knew that they would both be naked, and the only conversation would be about hitting spots and how deep he needed to go to make her cum.

"Are you gonna answer me?" Nova snapped.

"The fuck Nova, I answered your ass when I came in instead of leaving."

"That's not an answer, all that means is your horny ass wants me naked," she pointed at him with a scowl on her face.

He let out an irritated sigh, and stood long enough to roughly grab her around her waist. The second his large hands gripped her sides, he was seated again with her positioned between his legs. Rah hadn't played football in years, but you couldn't look at him and tell. He still wore every muscle, as if he were still a star athlete. He housed the appearance, like he spent every day of his life in a gym, instead of on the streets hustling. It was one of the things that like most women, including Nova, loved about him.

"Look ma, I like you. You're down to earth, cool as hell and of course this shit right here keeps a nigga fiending." His hands moved down her sides across her ass. "But that insecure shit ain't working for me. It's a huge fucking turn off. I don't give a fuck about that pussy ass nigga. He don't make my dick hard but this does." Rah lifted her shirt and planted a few kisses across her stomach. "So if you wanna let that shit fuck with your head, then that's on you. I'll leave, but if you want me to stay, then I suggest you let that shit go and make this about us."

Nova was torn. She kept hearing Logic's voice in her head and there was no mistaking what he was telling her by saying that the line had been drawn, but Rah was doing something to her. He had a hold on her that she wasn't quite ready to let go of. She would have to worry about the consequences later. For now, she reached for the side of her shirt, pulling it over her head. With her eyes locked on his, a smile spread across his face before she leaned down to kiss him. In her mind she was saying it was going to be the last time, but in her heart she knew it was a lie. Nova was playing with fire but couldn't seem to walk away.

-11-

Joy walked into Logic's bedroom, dropped her bags on the floor and then climbed onto his bed with him. It was early, and she was tired from having been up all night with Karma. The two caught up on what's been new in their lives, while over indulging on junk food which Joy was seriously regretting, because her stomach was currently doing somersaults. With it being Sunday, all she wanted to do was spend the day in bed with Logic. She was praying that he didn't have plans because she had already mentally prepared herself for a day of doing nothing.

"I missed you," Joy mumbled as she snuggled up close to Logic, wrapping her body around his. He smelled like a mixture of soap and cologne, which she loved. Once her head was resting on his chest and her leg was bent at the knee and thrown across his, she exhaled and then smiled, feeling like she was home. Logic kept using the term home in reference to his place while she was at Karma's, but being there now, she had to admit that she felt the same way. It wasn't about his apartment per se, but more so about his presence. Wherever he was, was home to her. Joy knew it and so did Logic, because he felt the exact same way about Joy. That was something they both had in common.

"Then you should have been here last night and you wouldn't have had to miss me." He leaned down just enough to kiss her on the forehead, as his hand traveled up her back, under her shirt, gliding across her skin.

"You said you had stuff to do, so," Joy shrugged.

"Yeah, but when I come home, I want you in my bed. It's all good though. I know you missed your girl, but I hope you got it all in, because it will be awhile before I let that shit happen again."

"Let?" Joy lifted her head so that she could see his face.

"Hell yeah let...did I stutter? I told you I need you in my bed when I come home." He looked down at Joy with a sly grin, but there was nothing but truth behind his words.

"I guess we'll have to talk about that," Joy replied, right before her phone went off. She sucked her teeth, but sat up to get it.

"Yeah aight, keep thinking that," Logic said and then laughed, in reference to the fact that she thought it was up for debate.

"It's my dad," Joy said out loud. The statement wasn't really meant for anyone but herself, because she was curious about why he was calling. She hadn't spoken to him since they had dinner months ago, but it wasn't like they were fighting or anything. She knew that he wasn't thrilled about her being with Logic, but the two of them always had a sort of "agree to disagree" type relationship, so they learned to be cordial, and just not discuss her personal life. In fact, the only reason why she hadn't spoken with him lately was because she knew that she would likely tell him about her trifling mother, and she didn't want to be stuck in the middle of that.

Joy glanced at Logic who was focused on the TV, before she stood to answer the call.

"Hey Dad."

"I need to see you."

"For what?"

"It's important, just come by and leave your little thug boyfriend at home."

Joy looked back at Logic again and this time his eyes were on her. "I'll come, but Logic will be with me. If you have a problem with that, then tell me now and I'll just pass all together."

"Fine, just meet me in an hour." Even though her father didn't want Logic there, because he wanted to use the advantage of having Joy alone to try and sway her, he didn't really care. He just wanted to let her know the type of man she was dealing with.

"Fine," Joy responded.

Joy ended the call and plopped down on the side of Logic's bed. She sat there for a minute before looking over her shoulder at him.

"We have to go to my parents' house."

It took Logic a minute before he responded, but when he did, it was clear how he felt about it. With an arrogant laugh being first, he spoke sarcastically. "I don't have to go anywhere and I'm not. That's your shit, so if you need to deal with them then that's fine, but I'm not fucking with either one of your parents like that."

Logic's first, and as far as he was concerned, last experience with Joy's parents was enough for him. He had enough shit to worry about, so adding her fucked up family to the equation, wasn't worth the headache.

"But what if I want you to go?"

Joy crawled across the bed, climbing over Logic until she was straddling his waist. She looked down at him with pleading eyes, before she leaned in to kiss him. He kissed her back, but then looked at her with a straight face.

"That don't change shit. I'm still not going." Logic gripped Joy's sides and looked up at her without changing his expression.

"Please, I don't want to go alone."

"Didn't he just tell you that he didn't want me there?"

"No," Joy lied, but couldn't hide her smile.

"You're a damn lie, I could tell from the conversation." Logic released one of his hands from Joy's side and pointed at her, which made her laugh.

"It doesn't matter; I want you there. We won't be long, but I don't want to go alone."

"You're really fucking up my vibe, you know that right?" Logic looked at Joy and shook his head. He would do anything for her, that was already evident, even deal with her fucked up family if that was what she needed.

"Thank you. I promise we won't be long. We'll be back here before you know it and then we can do nothing for the rest of the day."

"Wrong, we're having dinner at my mom's house later."

"Wait, what, no. They hate me right now. All of them... your mother, sister and cousin."

"And your pops don't hate me?" Logic chuckled because Joy was damn near pouting. "And besides, they don't hate you. I cleared that shit up already and if they did, they wouldn't let me bring you over there. My mom made me promise her that you would come."

"So you already knew, why didn't you tell me?"

Logic laughed. "Because you didn't bring your ass home last night and I didn't want to hear you complain about it for a whole day, but then you threw this shit on me so fuck it. Now let's get this shit over with, and don't expect me to play nice. They come for me, I'm not holding back."

Joy rolled her eyes and climbed over Logic so that she could stand. "Same for me."

He just smiled and got up. There was no need to even justify her comment with a response.

A little over an hour later, they were at her parents' house and Joy used her key to enter. With it only being her parents, the house was quiet as usual, so Joy called out in an attempt to locate them, well her dad anyway. She was secretly hoping that her mother wasn't home, because Joy really wasn't in the mood to deal with her.

"Dad, where are you?" Joy was on her way down the hall, when her father appeared at the top of the stairs. He moved down them, slowly with the look of disapproval, as the kept his eyes on Logic. Logic, of course, didn't really care. He was there for Joy and her father and his feelings were irrelevant to him.

Lionel passed by the two of them, barely acknowledging their presence but mumbled, "Follow me."

Joy grabbed Logic's hand, knowing that he wasn't the type to adhere to a command, so she moved, pulling him with her. She was just ready to get whatever this was, over with.

Once they were in her father's office, he stood behind his desk and lifted a large manilla folder, tossing it towards the edge of his desk.

"Take a look," he said, glancing at Joy first and then Logic, with a smirk. It was that moment that Logic knew exactly what this visit was about. He knew that file was about him.

"What's that?" Joy asked looking at her father confused.

"That is what you're throwing your life away for." Lionel didn't bother looking at his daughter because his eyes were still on Logic.

"What did you do?" Joy asked glaring at her father.

"I didn't do anything. Now your friend here, has done a lot. It's all right there. I'm sure he failed to mention half of the stuff that's in that file."

"Is that why you asked me to come here? So that you could tell me what a bad guy he is. Oh my God, I really can't believe you. I don't care what's in that file. I know who he is. What I don't know is who you are."

Lionel laughed sarcastically. "You know who he is? You know that he's been arrested for suspicion of drugs and murder, oh and my favorite, domestic violence? He apparently beat his girlfriend bad enough that she filed charges. Oh, but then she dropped them, likely because he threatened her, or beat her again. His mother was a prostitute and an addict—"

"And my father was a pimp, who turned her out. The fuck is all that supposed to mean? Those are just statements based on another motherfucker's opinion of me. Some bitch ass, righteous muthafucker, who feels like they own the right to judge me. I ain't perfect and I've done a lot shit in my life, but you ain't no better than me. At least I'm not hiding who I am, but your bitch ass is. You think that wearing a suit makes you somebody? You did research on me well guess what, I know about your ass too. I know about your twenty-two-year-old girlfriend and your four-year-old son. Nigga, don't come for me unless you prepared for battle. Now if you're done, you two can finish this conversation and I'll wait outside. Tell her what you want about me; it might change things, it might not, but that's on her, not you."

Joy stood there with her mouth open, not believing what she was hearing. Did Logic just say that her father had a twenty-two-year-old girlfriend, with a four-year-old son?

Logic felt bad about putting it out there like that, but he knew it was coming. After he met Joy's father, he knew that he was the type to play dirty. Logic also knew that he was the type of man with secrets, so he called in a few favors and had someone follow him. He found out about his outside family, but planned on sitting on the information. He didn't want to hurt Joy, because it wasn't really about her, but Lionel forced his hand. Logic kissed Joy on the lips and then turned to leave. He could hear Joy behind him, but he kept moving to let her deal with her father. Logic had spoken his peace and was done.

"You two are unbelievable. You and your psycho ass wife. She's screwing my ex boyfriend and you have a side family. Why are you two even together? I mean really? As for that stunt you just pulled, I hope you know that's the end. Between you and mom, I can't deal. Both of you need help."

"Joy, you really need to watch your tone, I'm still your—"

"Don't! Don't even embarrass yourself like that. You're not anything to me. You just proved that, and if you want to be a father to someone, start with the brother that I didn't know I had. Hopefully you won't fuck up his life. Don't call me, don't come see me. As far as I'm concerned, you and your wife can pretend like I don't exist, because I don't, not to you, not anymore."

Joy turned to leave, but her father followed behind her.

"You're ungrateful and you're going to end up in a bad situation. When you do, don't call me. I love you, but I will not be disrespected by you."

Joy looked back at her father and laughed. "You can't even see it, can you? You have no idea how crazy you sound right now."

Without another word, Joy left her parents' house. She walked to her car where Logic was waiting, and got in. He started it and began to drive. It took a minute before either of them were ready to speak, but he went first.

"I didn't do that to her. I have never put my hands on a female and I wouldn't ever, no matter what."

"It doesn't matter." Joy looked at him and their eyes met briefly, before she turned to look out the window.

"Joy, look at me," Logic demanded. "It matters to me. She lied, Myesha lied. We argued, she got pissed because she didn't get the reaction she wanted from me, so she left. She didn't have a bruise on her when she walked out the door, but the next thing I know, the cops show up arresting me for domestic violence. They showed me pictures of her with a black eye, scratches on her face and a bruise on her neck. It wasn't me though. She dropped the charges, because word got out that she had gotten into a fight with another chick I was fucking round with. She was the one who messed Myesha up like that and she knew it, so she dropped the charges."

"I told you it didn't matter."

"And I told you it does to me," Logic said.

"Okay," was all that Joy, said without even looking at him. She didn't really care. She knew that Logic wasn't that person. He wasn't Rah. There were some things that you could just feel in your soul about people, and Joy knew that Logic would never hurt her.

"You good?"

Logic looked at Joy and waited. No matter how crazy things were between Joy and her parents, it was still her family and Logic understood that. So her finding out that her father had another so called family and finding out from him, wasn't necessarily a good thing. Since Joy and Logic met, it seemed like her family kind of fell apart. It wasn't exactly his fault, but he was at the center of her finding out about her parents' secrets, so he had to take some responsibility for that. No blame, just the weight of being the reason for her discovering who her family really was.

"I'm fine. They are who they are, and I am who I am. It doesn't change anything," Joy said.

"It changes everything Joy. Don't think that you're not allowed to have feelings about that shit. It's fucked up, but that's still your family. You're allowed to be upset about it."

Joy didn't want to talk about her family. She was upset about it, but more hurt than anything. She reached for Logic's hand and once they connected, she interlocked her fingers with his.

"Don't ever lie to me."

There was so much conviction in her voice, that Logic could feel her soul pleading with his. She needed him to be the one person in her life that she could trust, and he was going to be that.

"Never, I promise."

And that was all she needed. She believed him because she had to. It was the only thing she had left.

*****

"Why you stressing? I told you, you were good. They're over that shit." Logic surveyed Joy's expression, which showed her animosity for having to spend time with his mother, sister and cousin. He hadn't really had a serious conversation with either of them about Joy, so he honestly didn't know how they would react. But, if they got out of hand or disrespectful then he would check them. On the plus side, his mother did request that Joy be there, so he assumed she was over it, even if Najah and Nova weren't.

"Because I don't really want to go in there any more than they want me to. The last thing I need is to get into it with the women in your family."

Logic rotated his body just enough to face Joy, grabbed her hand interlocking his fingers with hers, and then leaned in for a peck on the cheek. "Look, that situation was fucked up on both ends, but this right here, isn't changing. I'm in this. Are you?" The earnestness in his tone had Joy a little thrown. It was almost as if he had concerns.

"Yes, why would you even ask me that?" Joy scrunched up her face, disappointed that her devotion to what they had was even in question.

"Because this is where shit gets real. If we can't deal with the simple things, then when the complicated things happen, we're definitely not going to make it and we have to make it because this— you and me—is the only thing that I can truly count on. It's the only thing I believe in." Logic was intense but sincere. He understood that the two were different and that would play a role in how things worked in their lives. So far, it hadn't really mattered, but with his life changing, he needed to know that Joy was in this and that she had the heart to deal with whatever was thrown their way.

"This is what I want. You're what I want. That's not even a question worth asking, because I need you just as much as you need me, if not more. And that, alone is a guarantee that we're going to make it." The intensity in Joy's voice sealed the deal for Logic. He believed her, so with one last kiss, he opened his door and got out.

Joy took a deep breath, to prepare herself mentally, while Logic opened her door so that she could join him on the sidewalk. After one last kiss, and a moment in his embrace, the two climbed the stairs of Mini's house to face off with the family.

"Auggie, come play with us," Trent yelled from the living room, the second Logic and Joy walked through the door. As usual Trent was sitting on the floor, in front of the TV next to his cousin Kenyan, engrossed in the game.

"I got you in a little bit. Let me go see Grandma and your mom first," Logic said, as he shut the door and then placed his hand on Joy's back, to lead her to the kitchen.

"Hey Joy," Trent yelled from behind them, causing her to turn and smile.

"Hi Trent."

"You can't cook worth shit, so how are you gonna tell me what I'm doing wrong." Joy tensed up just a little hearing Nova's voice. She was really praying that things went smoothly, because if they came for her she wasn't backing down, and she really didn't want Logic to be stuck between her and his family.

"Hoe please, I cook better than you," Najah returned.

"Neither one of y'all can burn, so kill all that," Logic said when he entered the kitchen, with Joy a few steps in front of him.

It was like time stopped the second they heard his voice and turned to see him and Joy behind them.

Najah was the first to speak. "You been hiding from us?"

Joy looked back at Logic, before she focused on Najah again. "Hiding for what?"

Nova laughed. "She's just messing with you. Girl, wash your hands so you can help us."

"How you just gonna make her cook? Damn Nova, she ain't here for all that." Najah sucked her teeth and rolled her eyes at her cousin.

"No, it's cool. I can help." If they were offering a truce, then Joy was going to roll with it.

"But can you cook though?" Najah asked.

Joy laughed. "Depends, what are we making?"

Logic winked at Joy. "Yo, I'm gonna let y'all have this shit, where's Ma?"

"In her room caking with Luther."

Logic frowned at his sister. "Don't say shit like that."

Najah laughed. "Why not, it's true, Mini is hot in the ass."

Logic threw his hand up to make his sister stop talking, kissed Joy on the check, and then left the kitchen to go find his mother.

The second Logic left the kitchen, Najah glanced at Nova and then took a step to Joy.

"Look, I know you're probably feeling some type of way about us right now but don't. I love my brother and if you make him happy, then I'm good with that."

Joy looked at Najah and then Nova. "So the only reason why we're cool is because Logic told you we have to be?" As much as Joy wanted to be cool with his family, she didn't need them smiling while she was around and then going in on her the second she was out the door.

"Girl no, I don't have any issues with you and trust me, Auggie can't make me do shit. If I don't wanna fuck with you then I won't."

"We're good," Nova finally spoke up.

"Are we?"

"Look, I was feeling some type of way about the whole situation, but your past is your past. So I'm good on that. Rah is not a factor."

"Okay then, we're good. I don't know what you have with him but just be careful. He's not what he seems."

Nova laughed nervously, taking a quick glance at Najah before she focused on Joy. "Girl bye, there ain't nothing to be careful about. That's dead. I can't rock with somebody that's disrespectful." Nova tried her best to sound convincing, but Najah and Joy both picked up on the same thing: Nova was lying.

"Aight, well, I'm just saying. So what are we cooking?" Joy decided to leave it alone. It wasn't any of her business and Nova was grown.

"You mean what we messing up? Because this fool thinks she knows what she's doing." Najah rolled her eyes at Nova.

"Hoe, you got one more time time and I'm getting in your—"

"Getting in her what, Nova?" Mini cut her off when she entered the kitchen.

"Nothing," Nova said with a smirk.

"Did you see Auggie, he was looking for you?" Najah asked after sticking her tongue out at Nova like a little kid.

"I saw him, he's in there with Trent. Joy, can I talk to you for a minute?" Mini asked, looking straight at her with no expression.

Joy nodded and followed Mini down the hall to what looked like her bedroom. She shut the door and pointed to the bed.

"I'm good right here," Joy said defensively, which made Mini laugh. Joy was a little more, feisty and stubborn than she had given her credit for.

"Okay, I'll sit then." Mini sat on the side of her bed and then looked up at Joy.

"I love my son."

"So do I," Joy released with the quickness. That wasn't in question, no matter what his family thought.

"I know that, and that's why I want to apologize if I made you feel any type way the last time you were here. It was a bad situation and all I could see or think, was that my son had a gun in his hand and was not afraid to use it. The only other part to that equation was you. So forgive me if I reacted in a way that made it seem like I was blaming you. I wasn't."

"Actually, you were, but I understand why."

Mini smiled at Joy. "You're good for him. You love him, but I can see that you're not going to let that change who you are. He needs someone strong, who will be his voice of reason, when he's not thinking rationally. Auggie is a thinker, but when his heart is involved he reacts, which is why I know he loves you. He was going to shoot that man, in my house because of you. He didn't, because you stopped him—not me or his sister, but you did that. When you put your hand on his arm, it made him think, so I need you to be his voice of reason. I'm mentally sick every day just thinking about all the what ifs, but I know I can't change that. He's a man and he has to live his life so all I can do is let him, but I don't want to lose my son, so be his voice of reason. Give him a reason to come home to you every night so that I know he's safe. I can't do that but you can."

Joy looked at Logic's mother and for the first time, she saw the pain in her eyes, the way they were pleading for Joy to keep her son safe. Joy knew that she couldn't promise her that, but she would at least try.

"I will," was all she could say and with that, Mini stood, hugged Joy and then laughed.

"I don't know if you can really cook or not, but those two can't, so I guess we better go make sure my kitchen is still standing." Mini's confession about Nova and Najah made Joy laugh also, so the two of them left her bedroom heading back towards the kitchen. Logic gave Joy a strange look when they passed the living room, but Joy blew him a kiss to let him know things were all good, and followed Mini back to the kitchen where Nova and Najah were still going at it.

Nothing else needed to be said. Najah, Nova and Joy got cozy in the kitchen making spaghetti from scratch, because it was the only way Mini would allow it. Logic sat in the living room with Trent, Kenya and Kenyan playing video games, until Luther showed up and dinner was ready. The kids set up in the living room, while the adults sat around the kitchen table and settled in for dinner. The rest of the night was random conversation about a little of everything, and picking on Mini about the way she and Luther were pretending to just be friends when they were clearly much more. They kept finding ways to touch each other and were having private conversations, which ended in a lot of whispering and grinning. The night actually was a success and everyone seemed to be in a good place.

"So?"

"So what?" Joy lifted her head as she answered Logic.

He was stretched out on the sofa with Joy against his body, while his arms held her in place. His eyes were closed while she used the tip of her fingers to trace the outline of the tattoos on his arms. The apartment was quiet since they didn't have anything on.

"What did you and my moms talk about?"

"Our business," Joy said with a grin, even though he couldn't see her face because of the way she was positioned and the fact that his eyes were closed.

"Do I need to call her and ask her, because you know she'll tell me." Logic lifted one hand and went to go reach in his pocket for his phone, but Joy grabbed it to stop him.

"It's none of your business, just girl talk."

That made him laugh, because not even thirty minutes before they got to his mom's house, Joy was freaking out about how his family hated her and now they were having... girl talk.

"Oh, so y'all tight like that now?"

"Yeah, why?"

"Nothing, it's all good, but I'm still gonna make her tell me."

"She won't."

Logic lifted his head and frowned at the thought of his mother and Joy having secrets. That was a negative.

"So you have secrets and shit with my mom? You know I'm not having that?"

He slid his body from under hers, grabbed her wrists, pulling them above her head and securing them with one of his hands. Joy displayed a smile the entire time, as she squirmed to get comfortable under the weight of his body as he pressed his against hers.

Logic began with soft kisses to Joy's face, before moving to her neck, where he transitioned to sucking and tugging at her skin.

"You can't seduce me into telling you," Joy said before she closed her eyes and released a throated moan, that she was fighting hard to hold on to.

"You don't have to tell me shit," Logic said in between kisses.

"I bet," Joy moaned. She could feel his erection pressing into her stomach, which prompted her to open her legs and secure them around his waist. That was enough for Logic to take control. Within seconds, he was up and his clothes hit the floor. They were both naked from the waist down, and Logic's head moved down Joy's stomach, in between her legs. He dipped his shoulders enough to leverage Joy's legs over them, and then went to work. He kissed, sucked and licked every inch of her center, until he felt her body began to pulse and she mumbled his name.

Without missing a beat, he spread her legs wider and tapped her clit with the head of his manhood, before entering just the head. He knew that Joy wasn't fully recovered, so a smirk spread across his face as he watched her hands grip the sofa, while she tucked her bottom lip under her teeth, trying to control the wave that was about to hit her. Her sex faces were so sexy to him that he could climax just watching the pleasure that she was feeling.

After removing the head and then entering it again, this time going a little deeper, he kissed Joy so deep and passionately, that he could feel her energy passing right through his body. So with slow, steady strokes, he began giving that energy right back to her. The deeper he moved inside her, the more he was about to lose it, so he closed his eyes and just let go. Being with Joy was like an out of body experience for him. It wasn't just sex. Even if they were being rough, which they sometimes were, the feeling couldn't be matched by anything that he had experienced before, but now his slow and steady movements had him on the edge.

"Damn Joy, you got me willing to do anything for you as long as I know this will always be mine. Fuck, I love you, I love this."

"I love you too," Joy mumbled. She was in her own euphoric state so she was barely able to get the words out.

With that, Logic buried his face in her neck and began trying to reach the deepest part of her body, and before long, they were both screaming out in pleasure together. After they came down off their high, Logic lay there inside of Joy, kissing her chin and neck, smiling at the face that had him so wrapped up.

"I know it's a bitch move to say this, but I'm about to say it anyway, and I swear to God I mean it. This is my shit Joy. Don't ever let another nigga in it, or you gone have my ass in jail for murder. I put that on our unborn child."

Joy laughed. "Our child?"

"Hell yeah, they're up in this bitch tonight, 'cause I swear I just made it happen.

Logic placed his hand on Joy's stomach and had a big ass grin on his face before he gently bit down on Joy's chin and then her bottom lip.

"You better hope not, because neither of us are ready for that."

"Your ass might not be ready, but I'm ready. I'm ready for anything that's a part of you. Trust that." Logic spoke with such assertiveness that Joy couldn't even debate him on it. She just wiggled free from under his body and then headed for the bathroom. Logic was right behind her and after they shared a quick shower and got ready for bed, Joy decided to fess up about the conversation that she had with his mother.

"She wants me to be your reason for coming home every night."

"What?" Logic mumbled, half asleep, before pulling Joy deeper into his body and kissing her shoulder.

"Your mom... she feels like if I'm here for you then you'll have a reason to come home safe every night. She said she can't be that for you but I can."

"Mm hmm, she's right. You are my reason. You and this baby." Joy could hear the smile in Logic's groggy voice, but she knew that he was serious. She simply inhaled and let it out slow before relaxing against his body. If it happened, it happened, and at this point, she was good with it either way. After her eyes were closed, she let her breathing slow to the pace of his and shortly after, they were both out.

-12-

"Chill the fuck out Moses, I said I'll be there. Don't worry about where I am. I'm about to run and go check on Joy real quick and then I'll be by there. Let me worry about all that."

Nova stood at her bathroom door with her ear pressed to it, listening to Rah's conversation. She was expecting to catch him talking to another female, but quickly realized that it was his brother Moses, and even though she didn't catch him talking to another female, she caught him talking about one. She heard him clear as day telling his brother that he was about to go check on Joy.

Nova felt hot all over as she got pissed. One, because Joy swore up and down that she wasn't messing with Rah, and that her past was her past, and two, because Rah had lied also. He promised her, more than once that he hadn't seen or talked to Joy since the incident at her aunt's house, but he was casually talking about checking on Joy, like it was a regular thing.

It took her a moment to get her thoughts together and her head right, before she could face him. Her original reaction was to go off on him and then go straight to Logic, but she knew she needed proof. If she just went to Logic with some maybes, she would first have to admit how she found out. That meant he would know that she was still fucking with Rah, and she also knew that Logic would likely take Joy's word over hers, so she couldn't step to him unless she had proof.

She exhaled and then pulled her bathroom door open, where she found Rah sitting on her bed stepping into his Timbs. He looked up at her and smiled which she returned, but it damn near killed her.

Once he had his boots on, he stood, grabbing his phone off the bed, dropping it in his pocket before he yanked her into his body by her waist, and placed his lips on hers.

"I have head to the block to check on my brother, you good? You need anything?"

"Nope, I'm good." Nova pulled away and started collecting the clothes that she had on before Rah helped her out of them. She could feel him watching her.

"Damn, no complaining, the fuck is up with that?" Rah asked as he grabbed his keys off her dresser.

"I have to go pick up my kids and it doesn't matter anyway. You're gonna do what you wanna do, right?" She still hadn't looked his way.

"Don't be like that. It's just business, ma. I'm not doing shit but making money."

Nova pulled on a pair of jeans and then buttoned them, before she walked to her dresser to get a pair of no show socks for her Nikes.

"I know," was all she said out loud, but in her head she kept going, *you lying, cheating, no good ass nigga. I hope my cousin puts a bullet in your head right after he catches you with Joy.*

"I'll hit you up later and maybe I can swing through tonight after your kids are asleep," Rah said, oblivious to the fact that Nova was fuming. She was hiding it well.

"Yeah, do that."

Rah chuckled knowing good and damn well that she was trying to play hard, but wanted him to come back later. He actually planned on trying, but right now, his priority was Joy and then hitting the block for a quick minute to shut Moses up.

"Aight ma, I'm out." He headed to her front door and Nova scrambled to get her keys and purse. She walked out right behind him, locked her door and then jumped in her car. She didn't have a clue about following anybody, but she was damn sure about to learn today.

Rah pulled off and Nova kept her distance, following behind him. Luckily there was a lot of traffic, so she was able to get a few cars behind, but still follow his moves. Once they hit the highway, it was a lot easier. She got nervous a few times when it looked like Rah was slowing down, but he never stopped and eventually, ended up at a school. Nova parked on the curb while she watched Rah circle the parking lot. She realized he was looking for Joy's car and after he located it, he parked right in front of it, blocking her in.

Nova pulled her phone out and waited. About ten minutes later, a group of people walked out the building. She spotted Joy immediately and so did Rah, but Joy was deep in conversation with the group she was with, so she didn't notice him until she broke free and was on her way to her car. Nova could tell that Joy wasn't happy to see him, but Nova was prepared for anything, so she ducked down and waited.

The second Joy was close enough to Rah, Nova's eyes were glued to both of them with her phone recording, but things didn't go like she thought. She watched as Rah grabbed Joy's arm and it appeared that the two ware arguing. Joy tried to break away from him while looking around the parking lot, but it was just the two of them so she surrendered under his control. Rah had Joy by one arm and forcefully pulled her into his body, before grabbing her around the neck. Nova could tell that he was yelling until he finally let her go. He started to move away from Joy and then stopped quickly. Joy jumped and Rah pointed at her, yelled something else and then turned to get into his car.

Nova sat there with her mouth wide open after having recorded the whole thing on her phone, but what she didn't count on was being so caught up in the moment that she wouldn't notice Rah pass right by her. In fact, she didn't notice him at all until he slammed on brakes, jumped out of his car and was yanking her door open.

"You spying on me?" he yelled holding Nova against his chest.

"Why shouldn't I? I don't trust you and I'm glad I didn't," Nova yelled.

Rah laughed. "Bitch, I don't need you to trust me. You're not my damn girl, just some pussy in a rotation of many," he said through an evil grin.

Nova looked up just in time to see Joy speeding out of the parking lot, in the opposite direction from where they were parked. Nova knew she was in trouble because she had a feeling Joy was going straight to Logic, and if Joy had seen her with Rah, it wasn't going to look good for her; but unfortunately, that was the least of her worries. Right now, she had this psycho damn near trying to choke her.

"Fine, you want Joy, then let me go, why you still holding me here?" Nova looked around and still, no one. She got scared. It was like Rah had flipped a switch and had turned into someone she didn't know.

"Nah, it don't work like that. I can see that I need to teach your ass a lesson."

Rah raised his hand and smacked Nova so hard across the face, that she knew for sure his handprint would be there. He didn't stop there though. He had one hand secured around her neck and began to squeeze, until she was barely conscious. Once he saw her fading, he smacked her again, bringing her back and as she gasped for air, he laughed like it was amusing him to watch her suffer.

"See what happens when you don't mind your own damn business." Rah smiled as he lifted Nova's body so that she was upright. His hand was gripping her neck again, while he peered into her eyes, and Nova saw nothing but hate.

"Bitches always gotta fuck up a good thing. And it's a shame too, because I was starting to like you Nova."

He leaned in and kissed her lips before forcefully shoving her back, causing Nova to hit the ground. It took her a minute, but she scrambled to her feet backing further away from him.

"Tell your bitch ass cousin I'll be waiting, because I know he's coming for me. Especially now."

Rah winked at Nova before he disappeared into his car and pulled off. She felt a rush of tears hit, the second he was out of sight. She stood there for a second not believing what had just happened, and when she finally got it together, she got in her car and pulled off. She didn't know what to do next, so for now she was just going home.

*****

Logic massaged his temple as he listened to Joy ramble on about Rah showing up at her job. Truth be told, he hadn't really registered anything she said beyond the fact that Rah physically put his hands on her. Aside from her being upset, there were no visible bruises, but Logic was standing there in front of Joy with one arm folded across his chest; the other was bent at the elbow, while he stared at the floor massaging his temple.

He was so out of it that he hadn't even realized that she stopped talking, until she called his name to get his attention.

"Logic, did you hear me?"

"Yeah." He hadn't heard a damn thing she said, but it didn't matter because the end result meant that Rah was about to die. Logic reached for Joy's hand and once she was on her feet, his arms were around her. He kissed her on the lips and then let his forehead press gently against hers. "I fucked up but I'll make it right."

"Don't say that, this is not on you, and I'm fine."

Logic laughed arrogantly, before he stepped away from Joy and then around her. He walked to his bedroom, straight to the closet. It only took him a minute to have his gun out the safe and on his body. Joy watched, not really knowing what to say because she knew that it would be just words and wouldn't change anything. Logic was going after Rah and she couldn't stop him. There was a small part of her that wished that she had never told him, but she knew Logic well enough to understand that if she hadn't, it would have been much worse. She also didn't want to run the risk of not telling him and Logic mistaking that for Joy protecting Rah.

"I'll be back." Again, Logic stepped around Joy, moving towards the front door. She was right behind him and when they both reached it, he looked back at her with vengeance etched all over his face, and hate filled eyes. Once again, he pulled Joy into his arms and let his forehead rest against hers. He held that position for a minute and then kissed her lips. He didn't speak and it barely even seemed like his was breathing. There was a calm that washed over him at the thought of knowing that he was about to take Rah's life.

"I love you," Joy said barely above a whisper, once he had the door open.

With one last glance into her eyes, he stepped out the door and as it shut, she heard his voice, "I love you too."

Logic left the house with murder consuming his thoughts. His mind was racing out of control, but his demeanor was calm. He knew that he couldn't behave erratically or it might cost him his life, but make no mistake about it, he was on a mission. His first stop was the block where Rah's people worked. While he parked a few blocks away and waited, his gun was in his hand, first round chambered and when the opportunity presented itself, he was out the car and moving towards the block fast as hell. Logic had watched Rah's people enough to to know that the guy he was watching was alone. He came back behind this abandoned house where he stashed his product to re-up, so when Logic saw him moving in the shadows, he was on him like his life depended on it. He walked up on Rah's guy and shot him twice. Once in each leg causing him to hit the ground and yell out. Logic didn't need anyone fucking up his plan, so he grabbed him by the hoodie he was wearing and drug him to a nearby alley.

"That was just your legs. If you don't want to die, shut the fuck up and answer my question." Logic had his nine pressed against dude's forehead as he spoke, because if he said the wrong thing, then he was pulling the trigger.

"What question nigga, you didn't ask me shit, you just shot me?" he forced out, as he grunted through the pain he was feeling from being shot.

"Oh my bad, I didn't think you would cooperate, so I decided to offer some motivation for you to answer before I asked my question."

"Fuck you, I ain't telling you shit."

Logic shrugged. "Okay." He cocked his gun and dude suddenly got a change of heart.

"Wait, hold up, what the fuck you wanna know?"

"Where is he?"

"Who?"

Logic inhaled and let it out slow, trying to calm himself.

"Rah, where the fuck is he?"

"Shit, I don't know. You shot me because you looking for that nigga? Why the hell you didn't ask me that first?"

Logic was annoyed, so he ignored everything dude was saying. "I'm going to ask you one more time and if I don't like your answer, then you better say a quick motherfucking prayer to save what's left of your soul. Where is he?"

"I said I don't know, but he lives over on Briggs, a big ass brick house. It's the nicest one on the block so you can't miss that shit. If he's not there, I don't know where the fuck he is. It's not like he checks in with me. I work for his ass, not the other way around."

"If you live and I don't get to him first, tell him I'm coming for him."

"Who the fuck are you?"

"Don't worry about it, he'll know."

Logic walked away not feeling any type way about what he had just done. Rah could be held accountable. It took Logic about twenty minutes to make it to Briggs, and sure enough, he found Rah's house without any issues. He parked down the block and walked towards it, gun in hand, ready to take a life. As he approached, he could see a body on the porch, but he could tell from the build that it wasn't Rah. He didn't really give a fuck; whoever it was knew him well enough to be at his house, so they just happened to be in the wrong place at the wrong time. Logic walked down the block and when he got ready to pass Rah's house, he could see whoever was on the porch watching him out the corner of his eye. They had a blunt in one hand and the other under their shirt, where Logic knew he had a gun. The second Logic was close enough, he raised his, and hit dude right in the shoulder, jogged up the steps and kicked the gun out of dude's hands.

"The fuck yo." Logic's victim grabbed his shoulder where he had been hit. After looking down at him, Logic knew it was Moses, Rah's brother, which he also knew from watching them over the past few weeks. Moses was more die hard than Rah, always on the block and working with his people. Rah hardly ever spent any time out there.

"Where the fuck is your brother?'

"He's where the fuck he is. Why the hell should I tell you?"

Logic laughed. "Because I'm pretty sure your life is more important to you than his."

"Nigga, you sound crazy as fuck. I'm not about to send you after my brother, who the fuck are you anyway?"

"My bad. I guess it's rude as fuck of me to shoot your ass without a proper introduction, but what I'm curious about is how the fuck you trying to take over my shit and you don't even know who I am?"

Logic watched, as Moses gritted his teeth and sneered at him when he realized who he was.

"I don't give a fuck who you are but trust me, the second my brother finds out you were here, that's your ass bruh."

"You're talking big shit for a motherfucker that's staring down the barrel of a gun but yo, that's on you."

"The fuck outta here with that bullshit. I ain't no bitch, so I ain't afraid to die."

"I would challenge that, but I need you to live long enough to deliver a message to your bitch ass brother. Tell him to find me or I will find him but either way, his time is limited."

"What the fuck ever. You ain't gone do shit to my brother."

Logic chuckled before he raised his gun and shot Moses in the other shoulder, causing him to yell out.

"Fuck, you better be glad I can't get to your bitch ass. I put that on everything." Moses bit his bottom lip, trying to contain the pain that he was feeling.

"Don't forget what I said. Oh, and next time you think about the value of your brother's life over the value of yours, you might want to rethink putting him first. He don't give a fuck about you. He's fucking your girl and that pretty little baby girl that you're paying for is actually his. Your brother ain't shit. But don't worry, I'm gonna handle that for you 'cause I know you're not man enough to do it yourself."

Logic left Moses right there on Rah's porch bleeding, and walked back to his car. It was just a matter of time before he knew that Rah would surface. Once word got around what he had just done, Logic knew that if Rah was any kind of man, he would come for him and trust, Logic was going to be ready.

-14-

"Yo, I didn't expect to see you here." Gotti looked up at Logic as he spoke, but knew the second he looked at him that something wasn't right. Logic walked in, went straight to the refrigerator, grabbed two beers and then leaned against the counter, placing one on it, next to him, while he opened the other.

"Is there something we need to talk about?" Gotti asked, looking Logic right in the eyes.

Logic turned up his beer and after half of it was gone, he lowered it to his side and spoke. "I shot one of Rah's men and his brother."

Gotti leaned back in his chair, folding his hands back behind his head, making sure that he kept eye contact with Logic. "Not that I give a fuck one way or the other, because clearly I don't, and you know I'm good with whatever moves you make, but I thought we were sitting on this for a minute."

"Shit changed," Logic said before he turned up his beer and finished off the other half. Once he was done, he set it on the counter next to him, picked up the other one and twisted the cap off. Again after it was opened, he turned it up and downed half of it.

"Does that change affect shit around here or is this personal?"

"Personal," Logic said, before he finished off the second half of his second beer.

"Aight then. What do you need from me?"

"You're good. This is my problem, so I'll handle it. We already took one hit and I'm not willing to risk any more."

"I hear what you're saying and I can respect that. I can only speak for myself, but your problem, my problem. I don't really give a fuck. I'm down with whatever you need. I guess when you think about it, if something happens to you, then this shit right here is my problem, so it's all tied together one way or another, right?"

Logic chuckled. "Yeah, I guess you're right."

"Aight then. Just let me know and it's whatever. Since you're here, Marlo was released yesterday. He's beat up pretty bad but he's gonna be alright. I let Zeeno know to take some time, to help his mom get set up for Marlo at the house, and I figured you'd handle things financially.

"Yeah, I got them for whatever they need. I'll hit him up and let him know.

Logic was relieved to know that Marlo was going to be okay, especially after everything else he had going on right now. He needed to clear his mind before he went home to Joy, and that was going to take something stronger than beer to do, so he walked back into the kitchen, opened the cabinet and grabbed the bottle of Hennessy that he knew was there.

He only got one glass because Gotti would get high as fuck, but he barely took a drink. Logic on the other hand would drink, but he barely ever smoked.

Once he was at the table, he filled his glass, downed it, and then filled it again. Before he turned that one up, he shot Joy a text to let her know that he was good, would be home soon, and then placed his phone on the table. He had no idea how long he would be, but he didn't want her up all night worrying about him.

Gotti and Logic sat there not really saying much to each other, but not much needed to discussed. Logic was using the time to clear his mind, and Gotti was handling business. He was content with getting high while he did it. It just worked for both of them, until Logic's phone went off. It was Nova's number, but he wasn't in the mood to talk to her so he hit ignore. A few minutes later, she called right back, so he answered, figuring she might actually need something.

"It's not a good time Nova, what's up?"

"Auggie, can you come here?"

"Kenya, what's wrong baby girl, where's your mom?" The first thing he thought was that Rah had gotten to Nova for coming after his brother.

"She's in her room. She's crying and she won't come out. She keeps saying she's fine, but she won't stop crying and she won't let us in."

"I'm on my way, are you okay, where's Kenyan?" Logic rattled off questions as they popped in his head, not really giving her a chance to answer until he was done.

"We're fine, he's right here."

"Okay, make sure the door is locked and don't open it for anybody. Not even me. I have a key, so that means I can get in. So nobody, got it?"

"Got it."

"Yo, I need you to drive me somewhere. I'm drunk as fuck and the last thing I need is to get stopped."

"Everything good?"

"The fuck if I know, but we'll see in a minute."

Logic tossed Gotti his keys, and the two men locked up and left. It took them less than fifteen minutes to get to Nova's apartment and when they did, Logic let himself in. He found Kenyan and Kenya in the living room watching TV. Gotti sat down on the sofa while Logic tossed out questions and commands.

"She still in there?"

Kenya nodded. "Okay, you and Kenyan go pack a bag. Get whatever you need for tonight and school in the morning.

"Where we going?" Kenyan asked, looking at him concerned.

"To Aunt Mini's house. Go ahead," Logic nodded towards their rooms. He didn't know what was up with Nova, but if it had something to do with Rah, he didn't want the kids dealing with it.

After he walked down the hall to Nova's room, he tried the door but it was locked, so he knocked and called out to her.

"Nova, open the door."

"Auggie just leave, please, I'm fine." He could tell she had been crying; her voice was shaky and strained.

"Kenya called me, you're not fine, so open the door. Did that nigga put his hands on you? I know you were still fucking with him Nova, just open the door. I'm not mad Nova, I just need to see you and know that you're okay."

The room was quiet and then he heard the lock. Nova pulled the door and the second he laid eyes on her, he got heated all over again. Her face was swollen from where Rah had slapped her and she had choke marks on her neck.

Logic grabbed her chin and examined her face, but she snatched away.

"Sit down," he commanded.

She looked at Logic like she wanted to cry, which pissed him off even more. This was her damn fault. He warned her not to fuck with Rah, told her that he was bad news, but she let dick cloud her judgment.

Nova stood there looking stupid which was making matters worse.

"Sit your ass down."

"I'm not a fucking child Auggie."

"I can't damn tell. You doing childish shit Nova, now sit your ass down." He pointed to the bed, and she finally gave in and sat down.

"The fuck is wrong with you and Najah. Why the hell y'all keep fucking with motherfuckers who like to put their hands on you? Didn't you learn anything from her situation with Fez? Damn Nova, I don't get that shit."

"It's not like I knew, so don't compare me to Najah—"

Logic cut her off. "Why the hell not, you keep messing with motherfuckers that put their hands on you, same shit she used to do. Your father never once raised his hand to your mother, and I've never in my life raised my hand to a woman, so it's not like that shit is in our family. The fuck y'all be thinking? Dick be that good that you let a nigga do that shit to you?" Logic knew he was being harsh, but he didn't care. He didn't understand why they would allow that to happen.

"I didn't let him do anything and the only reason why it happened, is because I followed him when he went to see Joy. I watched him put his hands on her and when he saw me, this is what happened."

"So instead of you calling me when shit went bad, you decide to try and go up against that motherfucker on your own? You sound dumb as fuck right now. If I ever thought your ass was on some dumb shit, I do right now."

"I messed up and I know I messed up, but you don't have to come for me like that."

"Obviously, I do. I told you not to fuck with him and look at you. Have you seen your face? Damn Nova."

"I'm good, go worry about your girlfriend. She's the one who you need to be protecting, since it looks like Rah still wants her."

"She's good, don't worry about that. Pack your shit."

"I'm not going anywhere."

"Don't fucking play with me right now, it's not the time. Pack your shit. You and the kids are going to Mommy's house while I handle this."

"He knows where your mother's house is Auggie."

"But he don't know to look for your ass there, and my guy will be there with you until I can go get Joy."

"What guy, and you know Mini ain't having that?"

"She don't have a choice. Pack your shit so we can get out of here."

Logic left Nova standing there and when he made it back to the living room, he let Gotti know what his plan was.

"Yo, you said anything I need right?"

Gotti didn't hesitated. "Anything."

I'm taking them to my mom's house. Nova used to fuck with Rah and he's been there before, so I need you to chill there with them there for a minute and keep an eye on things. I need to run home and get Joy, but I shouldn't be long."

"I can do that, but you good to drive?"

"Hell yeah, this bullshit sobered me up real fucking quick."

Gotti laughed because he knew Logic was frustrated. Nova's apartment was small as hell, so he heard the whole conversation, including the fact that Logic's sister had been involved in abusive relationships.

The ride to Mini's house was quiet. Logic was in his head about finding Rah so that he could get get this over with. He knew for sure that he couldn't keep his family hidden away at his mother's house, but for now, that was the only option he had to make sure they were all good, even if it was only for tonight.

When they pulled up, Logic glanced at Gotti. "Give me a minute." Gotti nodded and relaxed.

After that, he turned to Nova and the kids who were all in the back seat. "Let's go."

Everybody got out and Nova had her ass on her shoulders, so she grabbed her bag and stormed towards the house. Logic got Kenya and Kenyan's bags, while they stood waiting. When he was done, Kenya grabbed his hand and skipped beside him as they moved to the house. Nova was already inside and Mini and Najah were both in the living waiting for him.

"Come on, let's go get ready for bed," Najah said reaching for the twins.

Nova had already gone to Najah's room mad at the world, even though she didn't really have a reason to be, in fact the only person she could really be mad at was herself since, everything that happened with Rah was her fault.

Once Najah was out the room, Mini stood there waiting.

"Don't look at me like that, it's temporary."

"You know what, I don't even care. It's not worth the words you're going to waste trying to explain." Mini glared at her son for a brief moment, without speaking.

"Gotti is going to chill here with you until I get back with Joy."

Mini narrowed her eyes even more, but didn't say a word. She just turned to leave the room. He knew she was upset, but at this point he didn't really care. It wasn't going to change anything, and he needed everybody in the same place while he had time to think. It was the only thing he could do.

Logic stood there for a minute looking around his mother's living room, before he left to go back to his car to get Gotti. The two climbed the steps, but stopped on the porch to have a conversation before Logic left.

"Lil Chris' girl just had her baby, so I'm flying solo right now. You might want to run through the block and check on things before you head back this way."

"Aight, I'll do that."

Gotti nodded. "They good with me being here?"

Logic chuckled. "Hell no, but I don't give a fuck. It's necessary. I hate that Rah's bitch ass is hiding though. That's some fuck shit."

"Yeah, I figured he'd come at you hard, especially after you shot his damn brother. I knew he was a fucking pussy."

"Rah ain't shit and that's why he's hiding, and he also don't give a fuck about his brother, trust me. But maybe he'll man the fuck up and show his face."

"If he comes here, you want me to handle it?" Logic knew that Gotti was only asking because he mentioned that it was personal.

"Do whatever you have to do."

-15-

Najah waited for Nova to start the process of getting the twins asleep, before she snuck out on the porch to talk to Gotti. Her mom was in her room on the phone with Luther, which meant she would be tied up for a while, and Trent was already asleep. She had watched Gotti move around in the background for the past hour, and she had done everything possible to get his attention, but he didn't bite. He didn't say much, or interact with them. He was there to do a job and he apparently took it serious.

Gotti looked up when he heard the front door open, and Najah stepped out onto the porch pulling it closed behind her. He was sitting on the brick stairs that led to the porch, smoking, and was about to put it out before Najah stopped him.

"Can I?" She held her hand out asking for the blunt he was holding.

Gotti displayed a cocky grin, extending the blunt her way, but before he let her take it from him, he pulled it back. "You smoke?"

"A little." Najah had burned a few with Fez, but it wasn't really her thing. She was just trying to find a reason to talk to Gotti.

He laughed. "You don't need this and besides, your brother should be back in a few. He might not appreciate me getting his sister high."

"You do know I'm twenty-three, right?" Najah snapped at the thought of Gotti thinking that Logic was her keeper.

"And I'm twenty-seven, the fuck age got to do with anything? Your brother is still your brother and I respect him enough not to get his little sister high." Gotti made sure he put emphasis on the word little.

Najah rolled her eyes. "Whatever."

"Don't trip ma, it's all good, and you're too cute to be smoking this shit anyway."

Now she was blushing, so she decided to change the subject. "My brother must trust you."

"Yeah, I guess so. Why you say that though?" Gotti took a long pull from his blunt, inhaled and held it in, before releasing a cloud of

WHERE MY LOYALTIES LIE 2

smoke. Once he was done, he dropped the blunt and stepped on it with the heel of his boot.

"Because you're here and he's not. If he's worried about Rah and you're here, then he trusts you with us."

Gotti looked Najah right in her eyes. "Do you trust me?"

She laughed. "Should I?"

"Shit, I don't know, depends on what we're talking about you trusting me with."

"That statement right there lets me know that I shouldn't."

Gotti laughed again. "You can trust me ma. I wouldn't do you any harm. I'm a good guy."

"Maybe, but I've heard that plenty of times before and I'm still single. One guess as to how that worked out, with all the so called good guys I've met," Najah laughed a little under her breath.

"That sounds like you put your faith in the wrong people." Gotti looked at Najah intensely, which caused her to look away.

"True, but too little too late, right?" She looked down the block when she heard a car turn onto their street. Gotti lifted the gun that was next to him, that she hadn't even realized was there. He gripped it, lowered it into his lap, moved closer to her, placing his other arm across her body and gripped her side. She knew the reason behind him doing that was so that he could push her behind him, if he needed to. The entire time he kept his eyes on the car, as it moved down the street. Najah should have been concerned, but for some reason, sitting there with him, she felt safe, so she didn't move. Once the car passed, Gotti relaxed and placed the gun back on the porch beside him.

"It's never too late." Najah laughed at the fact that Gotti picked up their conversation like it had never been interrupted.

"Maybe," she replied.

He chuckled a little before leaning back to pull his phone out of his pocket. He glanced at the screen and Najah did too. She noticed it was a female's name and she got a little upset, even though he ignored the call and dropped his phone in his lap. Najah was jealous and had no claim to him whatsoever.

"You can answer that," she said more to test him, than because she wanted him to answer it.

"I know I can."

Najah rolled her eyes, a little put off by his arrogance, but it was kind of sexy to her.

"Why you rolling your damn eyes? You know you didn't want me to answer that call anyway. I know your nosy ass saw the name." Gotti looked at her with a grin.

"Why would I care if you answer when your girlfriend calls?"

Gotti looked at Najah and chuckled. "You're funny, ma."

She looked at him and frowned. "Why am I funny?"

"You just are." Gotti noticed that she referenced his caller as his girlfriend, because she was trying to feel out his situation without really having to ask.

"Care to explain?" Najah asked a little annoyed.

He looked down the block and then back at her with a cocky grin. "Just because a female calls my phone, it has to be my girlfriend? If you want to know my situation, just ask ma. You said you're twenty-three right?"

"Yeah, so what?"

"Then stop acting like you're thirteen."

Najah sat there for a minute, a little put off by the fact that he called her on her own shit, but once again, Gotti's arrogance turned her on. She was about to speak up, but his phone went off again. This time with a different name. Before he could get his phone, Najah snatched it out his lap and held it in the air.

"Do you have a girlfriend?"

"Nope."

Najah answered Gotti's phone and placed it to her ear. "He's busy," was all she said and then hung up.

She watched his face, as he stared at her for a minute. She couldn't read his expression at first, but then a smile broke out.

"So are you taking her place or what?"

"Is it just a *her* or is it a *them*?"

Gotti chuckled before he snatched his phone out of Najah's hand. He unlocked it and handed it back to her.

Najah looked at him strange, until he spoke again. "See for yourself."

She started with his call log, noticing that there were several female names listed. Most of the calls were incoming. *Typical nigga.* After that, she went to his texts—same thing, a lot of "I miss you, come fuck me" texts, and naked pictures of various females. He watched her the entire time she searched his phone, all while displaying that same cocky grin.

"Wow."

Najah handed over his phone, which he dropped in his lap again.

"What?" he laughed.

"You might not have a girlfriend, but you're most definitely already taken." Najah looked him right in the eyes.

"Did you see anything in there that looked like commitment?" Gotti asked.

"No, but—"

"Then I'm not taken. You can change that if you want to though."

"You don't know me so why would you assume that you want me to change that?"

Najah waited for Gotti to answer, which he didn't bother to do. Instead, he just grabbed her chin and pulled her into a kiss. His lips were so soft against hers, that she melted under his touch and when he released their kiss, wearing that sexy ass grin that he seemed so comfortable with, she couldn't help but to smile back.

"Come on, let's go. We probably don't need to be sitting out here."

Najah wanted him all to herself, and she knew that wasn't going to happen if they were inside, but she also knew that he was right. The last thing either of them needed was to be caught off guard, so as much as she hated it, when Gotti picked up his gun, stood and reached for her hand, she accepted it. Moments later, she led the way into her mother's house and just like that, their conversation was over.

*****

"Where are you?" Moses yelled into his phone from his hospital bed. His eyes were on Alicia who looked like she was about to break out in tears again. She had been crying for damn near the last hour, first because she claimed she was upset about him getting shot, and then after that, because he confronted her about what Logic told him about her sleeping with Rah. Moses really didn't want to believe it, but the second he asked Alicia if Noel was really his, he could see it in her eyes. She didn't have to say a word, and if he wasn't laid up in a hospital bed with shattered bones in one shoulder and ten stitches in the other, he would have likely choked the shit out of her. For the past eight months, he believed that Noel was his, and she was actually Rah's.

"Why the fuck are you yelling nigga, damn?" Rah yelled through the phone causing Moses to grip it tighter, sending a shooting pain through his shoulder because of it.

"Because I got shot defending your ass and this shit hurts, so where the fuck are you?"

"I'm on my way there now."

Moses gritted his teeth. The last thing he wanted was to see his brother, for fear that he would shoot him his damn self.

"The fuck you coming here for. You need to go handle that nigga for putting me here. He thinks you're hiding from him, Rah. He called you all kind of bitches and he's got a whole team of people on the streets looking for you. What the hell you plan on doing about that?" Moses lied. He knew that Logic was indeed looking for Rah, but he had to embellish the situation to keep Rah from coming to the hospital. Knowing that Logic was challenging his manhood, was just the thing to keep Rah on the street.

"He can come for me. Shit, I'm ready," Rah said arrogantly. He meant it too. He wasn't afraid to die, it was gonna happen one day, but no time soon as far as he was concerned. He damn sure wasn't afraid that Logic was going to make that happen.

"Rah, use your damn head. I'm laid up in this bitch, I can't do shit. That means you're alone. You better get your head right because there's nobody out there watching your back."

Moses glanced at Alicia who was holding Rah's daughter, the daughter that Moses believed was his, and he started fuming.

"I'm good Moses and you can't tell me shit. Didn't you let that nigga catch you slipping? How the fuck you gonna tell me to get my head right? I ain't the one in the hospital."

"You're right. Well since you got shit all figured out, you need to handle business while I'm in here. We have a hand off tomorrow and if we fuck that up Drew's people aren't fucking with us anymore. We got too much shit going on to be looking for a new supplier, so you have to be there."

"Send Dee or Mike. Don't you think I have more important shit to do?"

"I can't do that Rah. Drew specially wanted us to be there. I'm in the hospital, which is understood, but there's no excuse for you not being there. I just talked to Drew and he said if you don't show, that's it. He doesn't trust anybody but us to do the deal. You know he's paranoid as fuck and he swears somebody's always trying to set his ass up. We need the product Rah. You have to be there."

"Fuck Moses, what time?"

"Six, and don't be fucking late. You know he hates that shit."

"You need to watch how the fuck you talk to me. The fuck you think I am?"

"Look, just be there to do the hand off. The money is in the safe. You know what we're getting right?"

"Nigga, I got this shit." Rah hung up and Moses sat there for a minute, before he was able to speak. He looked at Alicia, who once again was fucking crying. He really wanted to choke the shit out of her.

"If you don't chill with that shit, I swear, I'm gonna find the strength to get out of this damn bed and choke the shit out of you."

"I'm sorry, but this is a lot Moses. I'll leave him alone, I promise. I'll never even look at him again. Do we really want him dead?"

He looked at her like she was stupid. "Are you really sitting here begging for that motherfucker's life? Get the fuck out of here and when you're struggling, raising Noel all by yourself, don't even think to pick up the phone and call me. Rah is a dead man walking, whether I make it happen, or that nigga that's after him. He's dead, Alicia."

"No, I can do this. I want this to work. I don't care what happens to him. I can do this," she pleaded.

"Come here," Moses commanded.

Alicia looked down at her daughter and then back at Moses but didn't move.

"So you scared of me now? You just admitted to me that Rah damn near broke your jaw and yet you're scared of me? I've never put my hands on you since the day we met, but you're looking at me like you think I might hurt you."

Alicia thought about what he said and moved slowly towards Moses. She stood beside his hospital bed waiting.

"Sit down." He patted the bed next to him and Alicia obliged. Moses looked at Noel and smiled. No matter whose blood she had running through her veins, she was his. He had been raising her that way and it wasn't about to change.

"You did some fucked up shit and I'm willing to let that go. It's hard as hell for me to do that, but I will. All I need is for you to do, is this one thing. Do you want a second chance? Do you want to fix what you broke?"

Alicia nodded. She really did want to fix things with Moses, but she also didn't want Rah dead to make that happen. She was torn.

"Do what I asked then. It's that simple. You do that and we'll figure this out. I promise." Moses let his hand slide down the side of Alicia's face. She nodded, even though her heart was telling her no, but at this point she felt trapped. Life with Moses, who she loved, or life alone, since he made it clear that Rah was going to die. It's not like she really had a choice.

After Alicia left, Moses made a few calls as a backup, just in case Alicia fucked up his plan. As much as he loved her, he didn't trust her, especially knowing that she lied to him all this time about Rah. He really wanted to trust her and fix things, but there was a part of him that just didn't believe they could. If she actually followed through with his plan, then he would try. For now, that was on hold until he knew for sure.

Moses set Rah up. There was no deal with Drew. He planned on using Alicia to tip Logic off as to where Rah was going to be, so that Logic could take care of Rah. Moses then planned on having one of his guys there to take care of Logic. That way, he would could take care of both of them at the same time. As messed up as it was, Moses was ready to get rid of his brother. Over the years, Rah had done so much to Moses with little regard to how he felt. Rah was selfish. He only cared about himself and he had always been that way. He got what he wanted, even if he had to take it, and he didn't care who he hurt in the process. That was evident in the fact that Rah slept with Alicia, got her pregnant, and let Moses believe that Noel was his. Brother or not, some shit was just unforgivable. Rah had crossed too many lines and Moses wanted him to pay. Unfortunately, the only price Moses felt was acceptable was Rah's life.

-16-

"I hate this," Joy said, as she moved around Logic's room shoving clothes into a bag. He leaned against the dresser watching her, feeling equally annoyed.

"Hate what, Joy?"

"This!" She waved her hand in the air to suggest what he assumed meant the fact that she was packing so that they could go to his mother's house. It was a little deeper than that, but her 'I hate this' simplified her feelings about the situation.

After inhaling and releasing it slow, Logic grabbed Joy's bag, tossed it on the bed and then pulled her against his body.

"I know it's frustrating and I apologize for that, but right now, I need everyone in one place until I can figure out what's next. I'm not going to risk something happening to you or them."

"I know that, I just feel like this is my fault. He's doing this because of me."

Logic lifted Joy's chin with his hand and looked her right in the eyes. "This is not really about you, and it would have happened either way. He wants what I have, it just so happens that right now, that includes you."

Joy released a slight smile at the thought of her belonging to Logic. "You have me?"

He chuckled. "I better. I thought we already discussed that."

"I wouldn't call it a discussion, you just basically told me that I was yours, and that you would be going to jail if I didn't cooperate."

Logic laughed. "Nah, I told you that I was going to jail if you let another motherfucker sample what belongs to me. There's a difference."

"If you say so," Joy smiled.

Logic looked around his room and got serious again. "This is my life, Joy. I know you say you get it and you're in this with me, but I want you to be clear about what that means. There's always going to be someone who thinks they can take what I have. It comes with the territory. It's how things work and that means that you'll always be dealing with potential situations like this. I've never been the type to hide, in fact, I usually deal with shit head on and niggas don't like that, but I don't fear much—never have—and I'm not about start now. Rah don't mean shit to me, he's just another problem that needs to be solved. If he wasn't hiding, then it would have already been done. That's how I deal with things. I just need you to know that no matter what's going on, I got you. You might not always like how I keep you safe, but you will always be safe. I promise you that."

"I'm not worried." Joy said it with confidence and she meant it. She had no doubts about her safety as long as Logic was in charge of it.

A grin formed on his face before he leaned in to peck her on the lips. "Oh yeah?"

"Yeah, you said you got me and I believe you," she shrugged, and stepped away to finish packing. He just chuckled and watched since his stuff was already packed and waiting.

After a quick stop on the block to check in, they reached Mini's house. Logic shut off his car and looked around. It was late and things were quiet, but Logic still paid close attention to his surroundings, because you could never be too cautious. Once he had his and Joy's things out the car, they made their way to the house, where he found Gotti on the sofa in the living room playing Trent's game. He paused it when Logic and Joy walked in.

"We good around here?" Logic asked after he shut and locked the door.

"Yeah, it's been quiet," Gotti said.

"It's late, you might as well stay. Give me a minute to get her set up and I'll be back to holla at you."

Gotti nodded, and Logic led Joy down the hall to his old bedroom, the one that he shared with his brother until they were both out and on their own. He was rarely ever in it, because it felt strange to him, being there without his brother. For some reason, it felt like Bernard would at some point come walking through the door. As much as he knew it wasn't going to happen, there was a part of him that felt like it would.

Once Logic got Gotti situated and checked on everyone else, he joined Joy who had already showered and was in his twin sized bed, waiting on him. They talked for a minute before he went to shower and then climbed in bed with Joy. The two of them got cozy, Joy's back pressed against Logic's chest while he tucked one hand under her shirt, the other folded under his pillow.

"How many other girls have been in this bed with you?" Joy asked randomly, breaking the silence that surrounded them.

"None, why?" Logic admitted truthfully. He had never been the type to disrespect his mother's house by sneaking females in. Now he had snuck out plenty of times to handle business, but never in his mother's house.

"Yeah, I bet." Joy playfully rolled her eyes not believing him.

"I don't have to lie. I would tell you, because that was then and this is now." Logic kissed the back of her neck. "But you can be the first if you want."

Joy smiled. "Not happening. The last thing I need is for your mom or sister to bust up in here with my legs in the air."

He laughed. "We can lock the door."

"Not happening, go to sleep."

Logic released a muffled laugh because his mouth was against her shoulder. Joy moved closer into his body and closed her eyes, while Logic did the same and just like that, they were both out.

*****

The next morning Logic was up early, got Joy to work, and the twins and Trent to school. Nova and Najah were staying at the house because neither of them had plans, and his mother still wasn't talking to him. Now he was sitting at their spot across from Gotti, while the two of them discussed what's next.

"So this motherfucking is still hiding. That's a bitch move. First you come after women and then you run and fucking hide." Gotti was admiring the blunt that he had in his hand so he wasn't really paying attention to Logic as he spoke.

"It's all good, he'll surface sooner or later."

"What now?"

"Business as usual, fuck him. Shit don't stop because he's hiding in the shadows. Just make sure our people know to be on the lookout."

"They're good. I already let them know what's up."

"Aight, bet. I have a few things to take care of before I have to pick Joy up later. You good around here?"

"Hell yeah. Handle your business," Gotti said with a cocky grin.

Logic dapped Gotti before he stood to leave. Once he was outside, he checked his phone to make sure he didn't have any messages from Joy. Not knowing where Rah was or what he was up to, he told Joy to be in touch throughout the day to make sure she was good. He dropped her off and would be back to pick her up once her school let out, so for now, he was going to check on a few things, mainly trying to see if he could get eyes on Rah. It was annoying him that he couldn't find him.

On the way to his car, he noticed a car parked across the street and there was a female inside. She looked familiar and was watching him. Once her car door opened, Logic reached behind his back with his hand on his gun, not really trusting anyone right now, especially after he realized it was the chick he had seen both Rah and Moses with. She had her eyes on him and looked nervous as she approached.

"Um, are you Logic?"

"Moses send you here?" he asked, instead of answering her question about his identity. He still had his hand on his gun, which caused her eyes to move from his to the position of his hand, as she spoke.

"Yeah, but it's not what you think." She began fidgeting with the hem of the shirt she was wearing and adjusting her weight from foot to foot.

Logic narrowed his eyes at her, wanting her to get to the point. "Okay, so why the fuck are you here?"

"He said to tell you that, you were right about his brother and that he can help you find him."

Logic laughed. "So you fucking his brother and Moses is still cool with you? So much so, that he sent you to tell me how to find his brother? Get the fuck outta here with that bullshit."

Logic turned towards his car, but she kept speaking. "It's true, he would have told you himself but... well, you already know he can't, so he asked me to do it. You don't have to believe me, and I understand why you wouldn't, but I messed up with Rah and Moses is giving me another chance. He hates him just as much as you do, if not more, so I can tell you how to find him if you want."

"Nah, I'm good, and tell Moses his ass might be next."

Logic looked at Alicia with a smirk and then pulled the handle to open his car door.

"First and Prospect at six tonight. He'll be there. He thinks he's meeting his supplier but Moses lied. He set it up so that you could meet him instead. Moses doesn't care if he dies. It's the truth."

Logic glanced at Alicia but didn't say a word. He just got in his care and pulled off, leaving her standing there.

-17-

"Where's my daughter?" Moses asked after Alicia walked into his hospital room alone.

"She's with my mom. I hope you didn't expect me to take her with me, while you were sending me to set up a hit on your brother." She rolled her eyes, annoyed that she was stuck in the middle of all of this.

"You need to calm all that shit down, real talk. This is your damn fault. If you hadn't been so damn slick, sneaking around with that nigga, you wouldn't be doing shit but raising our daughter," Moses sneered at Alicia. He was trying real hard to give her a pass, but with her giving him her ass to kiss, when she clearly didn't have room to say shit, was making that damn near impossible to do.

"I'm sorry, but this is hard. You might deal with stuff like this every day, but I'm not you, Moses. It's not like I'm used to setting someone up to die. How do you expect me to feel?"

"I expect you to make shit right. You did this so fuck all that whining and shit. Did you tell him?"

"I tried, he acted like he didn't care. He knew who I was, so he didn't trust me."

"But you told him where to find Rah?"

"Yes, but I don't think he's going. I told you he knew who I was."

"Shit, I know that. That was the point. I wanted him thinking that I was so pissed with Rah that I was willing to hand him over."

"He didn't believe that though."

"Don't matter, he's arrogant. Whether he believes it or not, he'll show, just because it might be true. He'll be cautious about it, but he'll show. Any chance to get rid of Rah, and he won't pass that up. Trust me. What he doesn't know is that he won't make it out of there either."

Alicia looked at Moses confused. She wanted to fix this, but she also couldn't handle being responsible for someone losing their life. She did half of what Moses asked, but what he didn't know, was that she had a plan of her own. She planned on calling the cops and telling them that a drug deal was going down. She knew that Moses and Rah kept drugs, guns and money there, because she had been to First and Prospect with both Rah and Moses a few times. Jail was better than letting Logic kill Rah, and if the cops showed up and found drugs, guns and money, then they would arrest them both. That way neither of them had to die. She didn't want Rah to die, no matter what Moses wanted. He would never know that she called. There was no way he could, if she called in an anonymous tip.

She just hoped that Logic actually did show, that way they would both be in jail, because she knew Moses well enough to know that he wasn't going to be satisfied until Logic was dealt with, and if he was in jail, then Moses wouldn't have to deal with him. Alicia needed Moses alive and well. She had a daughter to raise and she had become dependent on the lifestyle he provided her with. If he was willing to raise Noel as his own, then she was going to let him.

"Why you sitting there looking all crazy and shit, Alicia?" Moses' voice pulled her attention back to him, so she forced a smile.

"Just ready for all this to be over," she mumbled. It was true. Not over in the way Moses was expecting, but still over so that they could try to move on.

"Yeah, well hopefully it will be tonight. Come lay down with me."

Alicia hesitated for a minute, but then moved slowly towards him. She climbed in his hospital bed with him, trying to be careful not to affect his injuries, but he still flinched and gritted his teeth when she positioned her body next to his. Moses kissed her on the cheek before she let her head rest on his chest.

"I'm trying, Alicia. I feel like we can get past this shit, but I need Rah taken care of first. Otherwise, I'll always feel like there's a chance that you'll fuck me over again."

"I know," was all she said.

"I'm not saying I'll immediately get over that shit, but I'll figure out how to make it work. I just need you to understand that if you fuck me over again, I'll kill you too."

Alicia felt her body get tense as Moses' hand stroked her hair. She believed him, and for that reason she knew that she would never cross him.

*****

"Rah, what are you doing here?" Maura asked the second she opened her door and saw Rah standing on her porch.

He of course ignored her, pushed past her into her house and sat down on her sofa. Maura rolled her eyes, shut and locked the door. She hadn't seen or heard from Rah in months, so it pissed her off that he just randomly showed up at her house without calling.

"Damn, I can't just stop by to show you some love?" Rah looked up at Maura with a grin. Him being there didn't have shit to do with her. He just needed a place to chill for a minute until he figured out his next move. As much as he hated to admit it, Logic had him cornered and he needed time to think. He wasn't used to dealing with someone who matched his arrogance and disregard for another's life. From what Rah could tell, Logic was keeping shit moving and didn't seem bothered at all by the fact that he was after him. Rah was the one hiding out and that was fucking with him, so he needed a minute to let things die down before he stepped to Logic. For now, he planned on chilling at Maura's until he had to meet Drew's people. He didn't really feel like fucking with the situation, but he also knew that Moses was right. They couldn't afford to lose their supplier and business was business.

"It's been months Rahjee, so don't walk up in here now like we've been talking every day and have been cool."

"We're not cool Maura?" Rah asked with a smirk, knowing that she was just talking shit. It didn't matter how long he stayed away, she was always glad to see him. That was why she was his first stop, that and the fact that they had no connections together, which meant that no one would know to look for him there.

Maura was a computer analyst. The came from different worlds, and should have never even crossed paths, but by luck one day Rah noticed her at the mall, got her attention and just like that, she was in love with thug from College Park. She always told him that he brought out a side to her that she didn't know existed, and he loved how classy and accomplished she was. Maura reminded Rah of Joy in a lot of ways, but he knew that she would never be Joy. At the time Maura was as close as he could get, since Joy wasn't fucking with him anymore.

"No actually we're not, so don't just show up at my house like we are." She placed one hand on her hip, adjusting her body so that the majority of her weight rested on one foot. Rah eyed her curvy body that was barely covered with just a pair of tiny running shorts and a sports bra. His tongue glided across his bottom lip before a smile crossed his face.

"You want me to leave?" He kept his eyes on hers while he waited.

"Yes." She turned, unlocked her door, opened it and then held it with one hand, while she pointed to it with the other. Rah smiled and walked over to her. His arm went around her waist, pulling her into him while the other pushed the door closed again.

"You sure about that?" He kissed her neck and then her shoulder before he backed her against the door, making sure she felt the swell in his jeans.

"Rah, don't," she moaned, as his lips grazed her skin. He ignored her plea, and before she could object, her clothes were coming off and so were his. She gave up and just let it happen.

*****

"Do you want to tell me why you're really here?" Maura sat down next to Rah and lifted the blunt he was smoking from his hand, placing it to her lips and taking a long pull. She only smoked with him, a habit that she didn't necessarily love but she enjoyed.

"I just needed to escape for a minute. You don't seem like you're complaining too much though," Rah smirked, thinking about the session that the two of them had just had.

Maura took another pull from the blunt before passing it back to him. "We never had problems in that area Rahjee. Now, commitment and respect are a whole different subject."

Rah chuckled and inhaled as he placed the blunt to his lips. "That shit just isn't for me," he admitted truthfully.

"I don't see why not. You can sleep with a hundred women, but does that really satisfy you?"

"Hell yeah it does," Rah burst out laughing.

"You know what I mean Rah. Are you really happy? Who's in your corner, who's really got you when shit really matters? You fuck bitches but you don't have a real woman on your team, or you wouldn't need all the extra."

Rah looked at Maura speechless. She was right. He didn't really have that *one*. He wanted that to be Joy, but he would have to kill Logic to make it happen. Joy wouldn't just choose him, not now. There used to be a time when she would have, but not anymore.

"I had that, but I fucked it up." He didn't know why he was telling Maura that. Probably because they were just cool. She made peace with the fact that she could never fully have him, so he was a play thing to her.

"Fucking around, right? You need to grow up Rah. You're too damn old to be so called playing the field."

He chuckled. "You want to raise me? I need guidance, ma?" He offered up a cocky grin.

"Fuck no. You're on your own with that. I'd fuck around and kill you. You like to put your hands on women and I ain't the one. I'll shoot your violent ass. It only took me once to learn that lesson."

"Bitches just be doing dumb shit—"

"Don't, don't make excuses because you're not man enough to deal with a strong woman. That's probably why your one got away. You're a pussy if you can't deal with a woman without putting your hands on her. Ain't no dick that good to let that shit happen—not even yours—and you got some good shit."

Rah burst out laughing. If any other woman had come at him like that, he would have gotten in her shit. It was like he couldn't help it sometimes, but not Maura. She got a pass. She wasn't Joy, but she was the closest thing to her. He just wished that he could let go of Joy enough to want someone like Maura. That shit wasn't happening and he knew it. So for now, he was going to sit there burn a few with her, maybe get up in her one more time, and then get back to business.

-19-

Logic walked into Joy's classroom, where he instructed her to wait for him, and looked around. He shook his head at how colorful it was, so much so that it damn near made him dizzy. From the artwork on the wall, to the ABC carpet on the floor, to the multi colored chairs, it looked like a bag of Skittles had exploded in there.

"Why are you looking like that?" Joy had been watching Logic, from the second she felt his presence in her classroom. She kept her eyes on him, up until he stopped in the center of it, with a slight frown that he hadn't even realized he was sporting.

"How can you stand to look at this all day? All these damn colors and shit are making my head hurt and I've only been in here for a few seconds."

Joy laughed as she stood from behind her desk and walked over to him. Once she was close enough, she slid her arms around his waist letting her hands press against his back.

"Stop, it's not that bad."

"Shit, yes the hell it is." Logic looked around again before he leaned in to kiss Joy.

She shrugged just a little, looking around before she focused on him again. "I like it."

He kissed the tip of her nose before he let her go and pointed at her with a grin. "You need to get your damn eyes checked. You ready to go?"

Joy playfully rolled her eyes, before she walked over to her desk to get her purse so that they could leave. She had been ready half an hour ago and was just staying busy, waiting for him to get there.

The two made their way to his car and once they were in and moving, Logic placed his hand on Joy's thigh, giving it a gentle squeeze. "Did you miss me today?"

"Nope." Joy playfully shoved his hand off her leg, which he immediately replaced and she didn't stop him.

"Oh, so that's how we're doing it?" Logic had his eyes on Joy, smiling, because he knew she was just playing.

"You were just being mean to me, so I know you don't expect me to be nice to you."

Her statement made him laugh. "The fuck Joy, I wasn't being mean. I was just stating facts. It's colorful as hell in your classroom and I couldn't look at that shit everyday."

"I decorated my classroom, so if you say you don't like it, then you're saying you don't like something I did, and that's being mean."

"I told you that's not being mean, that's being real and trust me, there's a whole lot of shit I do that you don't like, so I guess your ass is mean all the damn time." Logic laughed a little to himself thinking about the list of shit he did that irritated Joy.

"That's not true," Joy responded, trying her best to hold her smile because she knew he was telling the truth.

"So you didn't damn near cuss me out this morning because I walked in the bathroom to pee while you were in the shower? 'You could have waited Logic'," he said trying to imitate her voice.

His question and imitation made Joy burst out laughing. "No, I did not."

Logic stopped at a traffic light, put the car in park and then leaned towards Joy to steal a kiss. It lasted a little longer than the light, so when the car behind them blew the horn, they both turned to look behind them for a brief second, before Logic put the car in drive again and took off.

"You're a damn lie, but it's cool though because we both know the truth," he winked at Joy, which made her laugh again.

"I only said that because we were at your mother's house," Joy said to clarify.

"We're fucking Joy. You don't think she knows that? She knows, trust me." Logic looked at Joy arrogantly and she just shook her head.

"Where are we going?" she asked as she typed on her phone, replying to a message from Karma.

"I'm taking you home and then I have a few things to take care of. I shouldn't be long and then we can chill for the rest of the night."

Logic glanced at Joy, but then focused on the road again while he waited for her reaction.

"Things to take care of like what? Should I be worried?"

Logic placed his hand on Joy's leg again and offered up a smile. "You trust me?"

"You already know I do."

"Then you never have to worry, about me or anything else."

There was no way he was going to tell her that he was going after Rah, and potentially walking into a setup. There was no point, and regardless, he had no plans on letting anything happen. He was just that confident. Logic was walking into the situation with an understanding that Moses and Rah were setting him up, so best believe he would be prepared for anything. This wasn't new to him, so he thought the entire situation through. Right after his visit from Alicia, Logic left Gotti handling business on the block and he drove straight to First and Prospect to check out the location. The second Alicia released the information to him, his mind was already made up about showing up. However, he was smart enough to know that Rah and Moses knew that too, so he took it a step further to make sure that he would know what he was dealing with.

It was very possible that Moses wanted Logic to kill his brother for him, but Logic took it a step further and assumed that if that were the case, Moses would likely have someone in place waiting to kill him too, or to kill them both. Either way, Logic would be ready for whatever, and he planned on walking away from the situation the same way he arrived. He was just that confident about it.

When they reached Logic's apartment, they both got out. Mainly because he wanted to check things out before he left Joy there alone. He still didn't know where Rah was, or how much he knew about him, so Logic needed to make sure Joy was good before he left her at his apartment.

Logic did a walk through of his tiny apartment, ending up in the bedroom with Joy, who did the same thing she always did and began stripping out of her clothes. Logic watched, admiring her body, but also knowing that he had to leave soon.

"So you're worried about me?" Joy's question threw him a little, but he knew it was eventually coming.

"Always, but not in a way that you need to be concerned," he answered truthfully. Logic knew that he would never put Joy in harm's way.

"I know you don't think so, but I'm pretty tough." Joy looked at Logic with a serious stare which made him smile.

"I know you're tough, but tough can't do shit for you when you're staring down the barrel of a gun. All you can do is shoot or get shot."

"So teach me how to shoot," Joy tossed out like it wasn't anything. She threw her pants on the bed and watched the amused look on Logic's face while she waited.

"Come with me," Logic said as he admired Joy's body for a few seconds and as much as he wanted to force her against the wall with her legs around his waist, he had more important things to focus on. If she wanted to learn how to shoot a gun, then he was going to teach her. Joy followed behind him as he stepped into the closet. He rattled off a list of numbers and then asked Joy to repeat them to him, which she did. It was the code to his safe and once Joy had them right, he stepped back and pointed to it.

"Open it."

Joy paused and looked up at him for a brief moment, before she kneeled down to open the safe. Once she had it opened, she looked up at him as if asking what now.

"That's $500,000."

"Okay?" Joy said more like a question, trying to figure out why he was telling her that.

"Just know it's here. Grab that gun, the silver one." Logic pointed to the shelf at the top of the safe. Joy lifted the gun, stood and then extended it to him, but he stepped around her, back into the bedroom. She was right behind him, still holding the gun.

"You ever shoot a gun before?"

"No."

"Hang on." Logic stepped back into the closet and got the silencer for the nine she was holding. Once he had it in his hand, he walked up to Joy, took the gun from her, affixed the silencer and then handed it to her again. She watched without saying a word and once it was in her hand again, he stepped behind her, extending his arms down hers, lifted the gun that she was holding, and positioned her hands so that she was holding it correctly. His body was pressed against hers, and he smirked at how sexy she looked standing there in a matching lace bra and panty set, holding a gun.

Logic had his head positioned next to hers, as he bent over slightly to match her height, in order to help her hold the gun correctly. Because of his body position, Joy could see the smirk on his face as she glanced back at him.

"What?" Joy quizzed, trying to figure out why he had that damn smirk plastered all over his face.

"Nothing, you just look sexy as fuck right now, and I need to focus but you're making that shit hard as hell. You're making something else hard as hell too." Logic leaned further into her body.

"Um, if you want me to figure this out, then you need to focus," Joy laughed a little, which made Logic laugh too.

"Okay, hold this hand firm and squeeze through here. When you pull the trigger, it's going to make your body jerk, especially the first time, but try to keep this hand steady so the gun doesn't move too much."

"I can't shoot this in here," Joy looked back at him and frowned.

"Yes you can. I just put a silencer on it. Nobody will hear it."

"You want me to shoot a hole into your wall?"

Logic chuckled. "Yeah, why the fuck not? Shoot towards the bottom of the wall, right there. That leads to the field in the back so you won't hit anything, and the bullet will just get stuck in the wall anyway. You ready?" Logic asked as he kissed Joy on the shoulder.

"I guess."

He could feel her hands tighten around the gun underneath his. She aimed at the wall and then pulled the trigger.

The kickback almost made her drop the gun, but because Logic's hands were covering hers, she didn't.

"You good?" He chuckled a little because she looked frustrated.

"Can I do it again?" she asked.

"You sure you want to?" he asked with a cocky grin.

"You're teaching me because you feel like I need to know, so I might as well be good at it, right?

He smiled at her assertiveness. "Yeah."

Again, Joy gripped the gun and got in position. This time, he stuck his leg in between hers and used it to spread hers apart a little, until she was standing with her feet, shoulder length apart.

"You know what to expect now, so anticipate the kickback, so that you can hold the gun steady. This time, do it by yourself."

Logic placed his hands on her waist, instead of covering her hands, as she held the gun in position.

"Pull the trigger when you're ready."

Joy paused for a minute, but then she pulled the trigger and this time, she was able to hold on to the gun. It wasn't perfect, but she felt a little more confident.

"How was that?" She turned towards Logic, who grabbed the barrel of the gun, taking it out of her hands.

He wore a smirk as he pulled her into his body. "That was sexy as fuck, is how it was."

*****

"Is that all you do?" Najah asked after she was out of her car and standing at the bottom of the stairs where Gotti was sitting and smoking.

He smiled, happy to see her. He had left that morning before she was up because he needed to get home, shower and get back to the block. The two hadn't exchanged numbers or anything. Hell, he didn't even say goodbye, because it was five in the morning when he left and she was sleep.

"That bothers you?" Gotti asked as he watched Najah climbed the stairs. She stood in front of him for a minute, while he admired her small frame. She was short as hell, which gave her a cute, petite look. Gotti scanned her caramel complexion and almond shaped eyes, before moving down to her thin frame. She was skinny as hell, nothing like the women he was used to, and all he could think about was how easily he could toss her small frame around while fucking her.

"I'm not around you enough for it to bother me." Najah bit her bottom lip trying to hide her smile, before she climbed the stairs and sat down next to Gotti.

"You can be." He pressed the tip of his blunt into the porch to put it out, before he laid it next to him.

"I can be what?"

"Around me enough for it to bother you." Gotti grabbed her hand, and held it up to admire the multiple silver rings she was wearing on her small hand. He touched the tip of one which housed a tiny silver band that didn't go all the way down her finger. "That's not uncomfortable?" He was still admiring her ring as his large fingers twisted it around hers.

"No, I barely even know it's there."

He finally looked up at her, pulling her hand to his lips and kissing it, before he let it go.

"It must be some kind of style or some shit like that." He looked up and down the block before focusing on her face again.

"I don't know, I just like it. So you want me around you?"

"What?" Gotti asked looking Najah in her eyes.

"You said I can be around you enough for the things you do to bother me, so do you want me around you?"

He chuckled and looked across the street. "Does your brother know you're here?"

Najah got irritated that his answer was not really an answer and simply about her brother.

"Does it matter?"

Gotti glanced at her with a straight face but only for a second, before he was eyeing one of his guys across the street again. "Hell yeah it matters. I'm not going to kick it to my man's sister unless I know he's cool with it. Any other way is just disrespectful, and that ain't me, ma."

"I'm—"

Gotti cut her off. "Before you start that 'I'm grown' shit, I know you are. I'm sitting right here next to you, so I can clearly see your grown as fuck, but it's not about you. It's about me and Logic. That's my man before anything else and out of respect for him, I need to know he's cool with it. It's a code thing and I can't fucks with it any other way."

"So what does that mean?"

Gotti chucked. "That means exactly what I said. If he ain't cool with it, then that shit ain't happening."

"Fine, I'll tell him," Najah said.

"Nah, ma. I got it. I'll have a conversation with him if it comes to that, but first let me ask you something."

Gotti looked at her while she watched his expression turn unreadable.

"What makes you so sure you even want to fuck with me?"

He said it in such an arrogant way that Najah didn't really know how to answer. Truth be told, she didn't know what it was about him. He was sexy as hell and most definitely cocky, but ultimately, there was just something about his presence that she was drawn to.

"I can't really explain it."

Gotti laughed. "So you want me to go bat for your ass and you don't even know why you want to fuck with me? That don't sound too solid ma."

"What makes you so sure you want to go to bat for me?" Najah countered.

"You're cute as hell, stubborn as fuck, you love your son, and you've been fucked over by the wrong type of guy so much that you don't know what it means to have someone really want to be there for you and show up for you. A real man, and I want to change that."

Najah opened her mouth to speak but didn't exactly know what to say. So she just closed it and sat there thinking about what he said.

"It's cool. You'll figure it out in time, and I'm patient," Gotti said when he realized Najah couldn't say shit.

They both sat there talking for the next hour, getting to know each other. Najah realized that Gotti thought he was a damn comedian, always trying to joke on her, mainly about the fact that she was so small. He listened while she talked about Fez. Gotti already know that Logic handled him and why, but he kept that to himself. The two talked about their lives, sharing things that neither of them would have told anyone else, but for some reason they were comfortable expressing their innermost thoughts. This continued until Logic pulled up in front of the house.

Gotti glanced at Najah and then back at Logic, while they waited for him to reach the porch.

When Logic was close enough, he dapped Gotti and then peered at his sister. "The fuck you doing here?"

"Minding my damn business," she threw back.

Logic's eyes moved from Najah to Gotti. "This a thing?"

Gotti looked him right in the eye. "Yeah, you good with that?"

Logic paused for a minute and then answered. "Y'all both grown and it's none of my business." Gotti read between the lines; he was giving his okay. Otherwise, he would have flat out disagreed.

"You need to head home though; we've got some shit to do. Tell Nova to stay at the house with you and Ma until you hear from me."

Najah frowned knowing that he was likely about to get into something, but she didn't speak on it.

"I'll call you later," Gotti said and then stepped around Logic to walk Najah to her car. Once she was inside and driving off, he addressed Logic. "I won't fuck her over, she's good."

"I know," Logic said moving up the stairs to enter the house.

Gotti knew Logic's response, as simple as it was, was more of a threat than an affirmation, but he was good with that because he understood. Najah was his sister and he would always make sure she was good.

After Gotti entered the house, they both sat down at the table in the kitchen so that Logic could run his plan by Gotti.

"I got word on where Rah is going to be," Logic said and then waited for Gotti.

"So what we waiting on, let's go get him."

"It's a setup. The information came from Moses' girl. The same one Rah was fucking and got pregnant."

Logic watched the confused look on Gotti's face before Gotti spoke. "How the hell that happen?"

"She came by here earlier before I left. Said Moses sent her. The story was that Moses is fed up with Rah so he's tipping me off so that I can handle him. I don't believe that shit though, and even if it's true, I shot that nigga twice, so I know he's not gonna just let that slide. If anything, he's got someone there to take out me and Rah, or he's expecting me to handle Rah and then he's got someone waiting to take me out."

"Damn, that's some fucked shit, so what's the move?"

"I'm going. They have to know I expect it to be a setup. I'd have to be dumb as fuck not to, or they'd have to be dumb as fuck for them not to expect me to know it's a setup."

Gotti chuckled. "They are pretty fucking stupid yo."

"You right, but either way, I go prepared for anything. I've already been by and checked it out. It's a house out in the open, so you can see everything around it."

"Aight, what time we rolling?"

"Meets at six, but I'm good to go alone."

"Oh hell no. You're not about to sit up here and tell me you're about to walk into a fucking setup, and expect me to be like, aight deuces bruh."

"I can handle it and besides, this is my shit."

"I know you can handle it, that's not even up for debate but I told you, your problem is my problem and besides, if they shoot your ass, then I have to run this shit, and I told you that's your thing not mine. I'm good just like I am," Gotti said with a grin.

"That's fucked up."

"That's honesty."

Logic and Gotti both laughed and left it at that. They would handle the situation with Rah and hopefully, be able to get shit back to normal.

-20-

Rah walked into the house at First and Prospect and looked around. It was just after five and Drew along with his team were supposed to meet him at six. He was annoyed as hell because at this point, nothing he had planned was going right. All he wanted was to take Logic's territory, put a bullet in his head and fix shit with Joy. As crazy as it was, he was thinking about his future. What Maura said to him had him thinking. Rah wanted a family, a wife, kids, all that shit, and the only person he could see that happening with was Joy. He knew he fucked her over, didn't respect her or treat her right when he had her, but he was ready... well almost. He didn't know if he could be one-hundred percent faithful, but he knew he could at least keep shit from her and treat her like she was the only one. That's all she ever asked of him anyway. He could hear her voice in his head right now. *"I love you enough to be with you; the least you can do is love me enough to keep your bitches out of my face."*

He chuckled to himself, because he knew it didn't mean that she was expecting the fact that he was going to cheat, but that's how he was taking that shit. It was just a matter of time before he had her back and proving to her that he was the man she had begged him to be. It was funny how you could take shit for granted, but the second you realize that you're about to lose it for good, you want to act right and fight to keep it or get it back. That was exactly where Rah was now, and if he had to kill Logic to get Joy back, then fuck it. It was a done deal.

After grabbing the money out the safe and a bag of *loud* so that he could roll one while he waited, Rah pulled his phone out to call Drew, quickly realizing that he couldn't. He didn't even have Drew's number. This was Moses' shit. There was a time when Rah went hard in the streets and did everything, but after he got his scholarships, Moses took over. When Rah got kicked out for getting caught with a group of his boys, the dean's daughter and two keys of coke, he went right back to hustling. Since Moses had been handing all the important stuff, Rah let him continue doing it, put minimum time in, and commenced to collecting money and sleeping around. Shit just worked. Moses was on his shit, they were making money, so Rah left shit the way it was. It didn't matter to him one way or the other because everyone thought that Rah was running shit anyway.

Rah loved his little brother to a certain degree, but he thought Moses was a little bitch, which was why Rah treated him the way he did. Moses was too soft about everything, one of the main reasons why Rah ended up fucking with Alicia. He knew it was wrong, but he didn't really give a fuck. Pussy was pussy and if she was willing to give it up, then Rah wasn't going to turn it down. That was until she came up pregnant. She cried about Moses finding out, had a change of heart and Rah didn't care anyway. Since Moses was his brother, he told her to make shit right with him, pass the kid off as Moses and no one would ever know. To this day, Rah laughed about the fact that Moses was raising Noel as his own, and he really didn't give a fuck. As long as Alicia wasn't asking him to do it, he didn't care. The only person he wanted a kid with or that he would ever claim a kid with, was going to be Joy.

Rah sat down at the table in the center of the kitchen and began to roll a fat one. He was annoyed as hell and needed something to take the edge off. It was only 5:30, so he had another half hour before Drew was supposed to show. For now, he was about to get high so that he wouldn't be tempted to say fuck it and bail.

Since Rah couldn't call Drew, he called Moses instead. He didn't want to be sitting there wasting his time if Drew wasn't going to show; he had more important shit to do.

"Yo, what's Drew's number?" No hello, no how are you bro. Fuck all that. Rah didn't care, he just wanted to get this shit over with.

"What the fuck you need his number for, he'll be there, and if we running shit together, you should already have it." Moses got heated. Yet another reason why he was glad that Rah was about to die. He did all the work anyway, so why not collect all the profits. There was no point in splitting it with Rah.

"Just give me the fucking number. You sound like a bitch whining about unimportant shit, Moses."

Moses gripped his phone and looked down at Noel, who was on his chest asleep, while Alicia was sitting in the corner of his hospital room asleep in a chair. She would be leaving soon to supposedly have dinner with her sister, but Moses didn't trust that shit either.

"I just talked to Drew nigga. He'll be there. I'll send you his number just in case, but he'll be there. You just make sure you don't fuck it up," Moses yelled and then disconnected the call. He had no intention on sending Rah Drew's number, but he also knew Rah wouldn't call back asking for it.

Moses made a call just to make sure things were still going as planned. He needed this to work and he was ready for it to be over.

"Yo, we good?"

"Yeah, we're good. I'll be there just like we talked about."

"Aight, the second it's done, take the money—that's your payment. Take the money and then your ass needs to get the fuck out of there."

"I got you."

"Just make sure both their asses are dead before you go. If you fuck this up, that's your ass."

"Shit, I got this. After them niggas face off, I'm taking out whoever is left standing."

Moses chuckled. "Aight, I'm counting on it." Moses ended the call and placed his phone on the rolling tray next to his bed. He lifted his hand and stroked Noel's hair. She stirred a little as she sucked on her tiny fist. She had his heart, Rah's blood or not, that wasn't changing. Noel would always be his; it was Alicia he wasn't sure about.

*****

"He in there?" Gotti asked as he sat in his car, waiting to see if anyone else showed. The house kind of sat out in the open, so there wasn't really a lot of places to be there and not be seen. What Logic found strange was for this to be a neighborhood, it was quiet as fuck; no activity whatsoever. That had him second guessing them being there.

"Shit, the fuck if I know; there's only one way to find out though." He lifted his gun and chambered the first round. Gotti lifted his and did the same. They were both carrying glocks with silencers from their disposable stash, so that they could get rid of them when the job was done. Dressed down in all black, they both had latex gloves on their hands so that no connection could be made between them, this location, or the weapons they used. Standard operating shit, but necessary nonetheless.

"What if this shit really is a set up?" Gotti asked looking around.

"No what ifs, it is a fucking setup. We both know that, but because we do, we're good. Eyes open and pay attention to everything. Don't underestimate shit when we're in there. You got my back and I got yours. I'm tired of fucking around with Rah's pussy ass."

Gotti chuckled. "I feel you. We got this shit, trust that. First eyes on him, just shoot that motherfucker and if we get in there and shit don't feel right, we bail."

Logic nodded and raised a closed fist to Gotti, which he met with his. They both got out and prepared to go handle Rah. Placing his gun under his shirt, the first thing that came to mind was Joy. He would kill a thousand niggas if it meant that she would always be his. That, he was sure of. And for that reason alone, he knew that he had to make it out of this, no matter what.

*****

"Are you sure you want to do this?" Tracy looked at her sister and frowned. She didn't understand why Alicia was even getting involved in any of this. She could leave Moses and walk away clean. If she made that call, she ran the risk of putting her own life in danger. What if they didn't arrest Rah, or whoever this Logic person was, for that matter. And then there was Moses. If the cops showed up because of an anonymous tip, he would know that it was because of her. She was the only one who knew that he was setting Rah up.

"Yes I'm sure, stop asking me that, damn Tracy."

"Just leave him. You'll be fine, you'll figure things out without him. I'll help you, but if either one of them finds out you set them up to be arrested, don't you think they'll come for you? Think about Noel, Alicia."

"I am thinking about Noel. I can't have her father killed. I don't want to be with him, but Rah is still her father Tracy."

The name Rah caught Nova's attention. She hadn't been on her shift for ten minutes and she was hearing Rah's name. She was a few feet away from the table where two women she didn't know were talking. One of them had a baby in a car seat next to her, and they were discussing Rah. She decided to listen, not really sure why, but she did.

"You sound stupid, Alicia. He's a fucking sperm donor. He doesn't care 'bout Noel or you. Didn't that nigga tell you to let Moses think that she was his? Who does that? What father does that? Don't try to save him. It's not worth it, and you know that Moses will come for you. Just stay out of it. Let them do what they're going to do and leave it alone."

"I can't do that Tracy. If this Logic guy gets there and finds Rah, he's going to kill him."

"Didn't he act like he didn't care, that he didn't trust you enough to even go?"

"Yeah, but Moses thinks he will. I can't let him kill Rah. I just can't do that."

"So you think the right thing to do is call the cops and tip them off about a drug deal? What if they just so happen to not have drugs there when the cops show up, and they can't arrest anybody? Logic knows you told him to go, Moses knows you knew about it. Everything points back to you. Just leave it alone and stay out of it."

Nova felt her heart racing. Not only was this chick talking about Rah, she was also talking about Logic and tipping the cops off about a drug deal. Nova didn't have all the details, but she wasn't about to let her cousin go to jail.

Alicia lifted her phone from the table they were sitting at, keyed the code to make her number show up private to her caller, and dialed. "Is this Detective Parks?"

"It is, who's speaking please?"

"I can't tell you my name, but I have some information for you."

"Oh yeah, what's that?"

"I'll tell you, but you have to promise to take it serious. If not, someone is going to die."

"Okay, I'm listening," Detectives Parks said. He was intrigued by his caller.

"Promise me first that you'll take it serious."

"I will, you have my word. Are you sure you don't want to tell me who you are?"

"I'm sure."

"Okay, what's going on?"

"There's a drug deal going down. A big one, and if you don't show up, someone will die."

"And how do you know this?" Parks asked.

"My boyfriend was talking about it. I don't want him to go to jail, but I don't want him to die either so you have to go."

"And where is all this supposed to take place?"

"First and Prospect, six o'clock." Now Parks was really curious. He stood and was grabbing his keys. They had been watching a house on First and Prospect for a few months, trying to get the timing down to catch Drew after being tipped off to him supplying some brothers there. There was no word about this delivery that she was talking about, but it wouldn't hurt to check it out, so he was heading there now.

"That's in less than a half hour, Miss. I don't know if I can get there in time, and you do understand we take this very serious, so if this is a—"

"It's not, I promise you it's not, just get there and you'll see."

"Okay, but I need a way to contact you."

"No."

Alicia hung up and looked at her skier who was shaking her head.

"You just fucked up and you can't take that back. I hope you know what you're doing."

*****

Najah looked at the clock on the wall of IHOP and cussed. "Fuck." *5:38.* She really wanted to snatch a hole in this bitch for setting her cousin up, but right now she had to find him and make sure he didn't show up to this damn First and Prospect.

Within seconds, Nova had her phone in her hand dialing Logic. His phone went straight to voicemail, so she called Najah.

"Aye boo, I thought you were at work."

"I am. Didn't you say that Gotti told you he had something to handle with Logic before you left them?"

"Yea, why?"

"Call him. It's a fucking setup."

"What do you mean it's a setup?"

"Long story, but I just overheard this bitch in her tipping off the cops about where a during deal was going down. Auggie thinks he's going there to get Rah, but this bitch is sending the cops. Call Gotti. Auggie won't answer, his phone keeps going straight to voicemail. We can't let him go to jail Nah Nah.

"Aight bye, I'm calling him now."

Nova walked in the back and grabbed her purse. Her manager looked at her pissed, but Nova ignored her.

"Where do you think you're going?" she asked following behind Nova.

"Family emergency."

"Don't you think you need to clear that with me first?"

Nova spun on her heels and spoke without thinking first. She needed her job, but she needed her family even more and she wasn't about to let Logic go to jail, so work wasn't the move right now.

"Bitch, you sound crazy. I know you heard me say family emergency. How the fuck am I supposed to clear that with you?" Nova turned and walked back into the restaurant.

"If you leave, don't come back."

Nova didn't even acknowledge her. Instead, she walked over to Alicia and her sister.

"What's your name?" she asked looking right at Alicia.

"Alicia, why?"

Nova punched her dead in her eye and then pointed at her. "If my cousin goes to jail because of your dumb ass, I will find you and fuck you up. That black eye will be the least of your worries."

With that, Nova left her job heading to her aunt's house where Najah was. She was praying that Najah could at least get Gotti on the phone, to stop them before they got there, because if not, this situation was about to go all kinds of wrong. Once she was in her car, she burned out of the parking lot trying Logic's phone again, over and over again, like he would somehow magically pick up. She knew the game. Phones were a distraction, so when he handled business it was off. Her only hope was that Najah could reach Gotti. She had to because Logic going to jail just wasn't an option.

To Be Continued...

Join our mailing list to get a notification when Leo Sullivan Presents has another release!

Text **LEOSULLIVAN** to **22828** to join!

To submit a manuscript for our review, email us at leosullivanpresents@gmail.com

CPSIA information can be obtained
at www.ICGtesting.com
Printed in the USA
LVOW04s2355130616

492399LV00029B/845/P